Big Bear Tales
A Collection of Short Stories
By Four Big Bear Authors

Lori Brookes
Karene Horst
Yvonne Phillips
Christie Walker Bos

flying trees publishing

DEDICATION

"To all those who have lived and loved Big Bear
and the surrounding San Bernardino Mountains."

TABLE OF CONTENTS

INTRODUCTION

What prompted four Big Bear authors to collaborate on a collection of short stories and anecdotal tales? It all started with a question from our readers ... "Do you have stories about Big Bear?" Now the answer is a resounding, Yes!

Within the pages of *Big Bear Tales*, you'll find a wide variety of stories including pure fiction such as Yvonne Phillips' *A Click Away* or Karene Horst's nonfiction piece *Snakes I Have Known and Loved*; read Lori Brookes' story based on her post as a fire lookout tower volunteer in *Where There's Smoke* or enjoy a blending of shared Big Bear experiences in Christie Walker Bos' fictional story, *Power Outage.*

Whether you prefer fiction, nonfiction, or fiction based on real events, *Big Bear Tales* has something for every reader. So, sit back, relax, and be prepared to be transported down ski slopes, through the trees, up mountains, and into the lives of people connected to the Big Bear Valley experience.

AFTER THE FIRES
Lori Brookes

    Fire. Destruction. Loss. Devastation. Grief. Acceptance. Rebirth. So goes that cycle during and after the fires. Both the literal kind of fires of treasured forested wildlands, and the metaphorical ones, that every one of us experiences during this lovely, sometimes painful, experiment of a journey called life.

Living in Southern California, with all of its sun-shiny days, brings with it a unique challenge in the area of our arid landscapes, leading to its vulnerability from both human causes, whether accidental or purposeful, and natural occurrences of the dreaded wildland fires. For those of us who dwell here, this is a daily mindful exercise of heeding Smokey Bear's mantra.

* * *

The forecast for June 19, 2017: Nothing but blue skies, which is the 320+ day norm for Big Bear Lake, no 'June Gloom' here!

My forecast for the day was a lovely solo hike, which I take often, out on my favorite section of the Pacific Crest Trail (PCT). As a little refresher, the PCT is what they call a thru-hike that begins at the border of Mexico (the Southern Terminus) and ends at the Canadian border (the Northern Terminus). Approximately 2,650 miles in length, navigating through the highs and lows of California, Oregon, and Washington State, referring not only to the geography but seasonal temperatures as well. The trail which was conceptualized in 1932 and decades later in 1968 was authorized by Congress as the Pacific Crest National Scenic Trail. The entire route, a major undertaking as you can imagine, was finalized in 1972 and completed in 1993.

You may be somewhat familiar with the trail as it was popularized through Cheryl Strayed's memoir "Wild" or perhaps you may have taken the epic journey to trek it yourself. If so, kudos to you my adventurous friend!

In our Big Bear Valley, we are blessed to have some 30 miles dedicated to the PCT and you will find many of us hiker types out on the sections (the intervals between roads as they are called) all year round. And during thru-hiking season our wonderful community of Big Bearians is happily shuttling, sheltering, feeding, and chatting it up with our transitory guests from all over the nation and the world.

My favorite section of the PCT, so far, begins across from the large dirt parking area on the East end of the valley, located at the crest of Hwy. 18, also known as Cushenberry Grade, ending at Holcomb Valley Road and the Transfer Station (a polite term for our local dump). Four miles out-and-back, forested with native pines, serviceberries, mountain mahogany, twisted bark junipers, and the surprising display of Joshua trees. This is where the geological lines of flora and fauna start their blend on the palette of mountain and desert. My boots crunched on the path layered with fallen pine needles, each step releasing the 'this is why I moved to the mountains' scent,' mixed with earthy wafts of scrubby sage and rabbitbrush. It's a present-moment, full-body, and mind sensory experience. *This* never gets old! Did I mention it was a bluebird day?

About one mile in, and if you blink you might miss this. There is an opening off the trail to the right, with a hint of something peeking around the trees. Keep going and there it is! The Zen bench. That's what I call it anyway. Someone has built a long seat using two tree stumps and a simple plank of wood. Buried inside one of the stumps, hollowed over time, is a Pringles chip canister. My first thought was, "How rude! Someone has left their trash in here." But after popping the lid, still intact, revealed a tightly rolled up journal and a pen. Ah hah! It's a geocache. Often found at hiking destinations, like mountaintops, but this one was right here at the Zen bench, the journal is scribed with many 'I was here!' kinds of messages, dates, Instagram names to follow on social media, and so on.

As always, drawn to lines on a blank page, I follow suit and make my indelible mark. I was here! [dated]

6/19/17. Now, let us turn our attention to the Zen of it all. Sitting cross-legged and looking easterly, the distant sfumato desert views, resembling the painted scenes scrolling by while riding the Disneyland Railroad, the train to flop on when your barking dogs just can't go another goofy step.

Breathe. Breathe it all in. How lucky am I to live in this wonderland of bountiful beauty.

Time to keep moving. I'm back on the trail, feeling even lighter after the Zen bench stop. The path is ever-winding, and around each curve another gorgeous display of Mother Nature's handiwork. Feelings of gratitude for the soles tied tightly to my feet. Closing in on the end of this trail section, looking forward to the delightful view of the red-orange rock that sneaks through tops of pines, juxtaposing typically blue skies, I call it the notch. It's the entrance to an old mining site. But something feels amiss. Smoke! I smell smoke. And, that's never a good thing!

I pick up my pace and now I see the smoke, the familiar color of the notch is obscured by thick gray-to-black plumes. Racing closer, I see flames through the black smoke, across Holcomb Valley Road. The mountain is clearly on fire.

As a trained U.S. Forest Service Fire Lookout Volunteer, I stop to gather the GPS coordinates to make *that* call into dispatch, but thankfully I hear the screaming sirens of the first responders. Rattled to my core and heart pounding, my head is still about my shoulders. I turn and leave the scene and make my way, ever so quickly, the two long miles back to my car.

The fire, known as the Holcomb Fire, today remains 'under investigation', however, there is speculation/rumors that it was of human cause, likely an illegal campfire near the PCT off Holcomb Valley Road or the Doble Trail Camp in the same vicinity.

After four days of valiant and combined efforts of 1,200 firefighters, from the United States Forest Service, Bureau of Land Management, San Bernardino County, CAL FIRE, and our local heroes at the Big Bear Fire Department, the 1,503-acre fire was contained. They were on it! Enduring higher than average weather temperatures and always the high wind factor, the incident brought 104 fire engines, 10 water tenders, 25 hand crews, 1 air tanker, 2 planes, 7 helicopters, and 6 bulldozers to the area's rescue. Two fire personnel sustained non-life-threatening injuries. Much respect and much gratitude for these heroic men and women in our fire service community.

The affected area went into a Forest Closure Order, by the authority of the Forest Service: No. 05-12-51-17-01, Holcomb Fire Closure, from July 1, 2017, through June 30, 2018. This included the popular short forest service road, used by the off-roading community, known as Jacoby Canyon Road or 3N61. Jacoby Canyon Road remains closed to vehicular use under another order that went into effect from December 2022 through November 2023. At the time of this writing, those dates have not been updated.

Why am I bringing up Jacoby Canyon? Because you never know when and where magical things will happen!

Along with my service as a Fire Lookout Volunteer, I'm also a Trail Steward for the San Bernardino National Forest. Trained for trail maintenance, including cutting trees, the overgrowth after long wet seasons, trail cutting, rerouting, and much more.

* * *

One year after the smoldering subsided from the Holcomb Fire, and the rain events that followed, I was out on a surveillance mission on Jacoby Canyon Road, on foot. Assessing the fire damage to trees, taking note of those hazardous charred skeletons within fall range of the road itself. The deeper we went the more we saw, not only the blackened state of the forest but the road itself. The rains had widened the stream and carved away portions of the road with the wetlands feeding the willows into a tangled weave of obstruction. What a mess!

While taking notes and pictures with GPS coordinates, I stumbled across quite the showstopper! There it was, amongst the devastation, the broad stroke canvas of spindly black trees—a lone sunflower was growing up out of the ashes of the charred landscape. Being an absolute nut job for metaphors, this was over-the-top with symbology. I could hardly contain myself!

I wielded my camera in this new direction and as any good photographer does and I started shooting endlessly. Every imaginable angle; up high, down low, vertical, horizontal, wide lens, up close, a virtual 360º of click, click, click. I knew the moment I saw this

lone beauty I had something. Big category—
'something' is, and that something would have to
wait and would be determined later as I had more to
document along this disjointed road.

Now the fun begins as I empty and separate the day's
photos into two folders on my computer: the forestry
work and my OMG moment with the sunflower.
Hours pass in the post-production processing of my
glowing golden beauty, poised in the middle of
nothing but charred reminders of the once thriving
forest—it's nothing short of a stark living contrast.

I settle on 'the one' after shuffling through the many
poses. Now what? I so wanted to share this image
with someone, or the whole world. There was much
meaning here and I was sunstruck, in absolute awe
over this event I had witnessed. During my career as
a graphic designer and creative director, I was in
search of a way to use this image in my client work,
perhaps an advertising campaign, or… I don't know,
somewhere! It was just too good, in my humble
opinion, not to find the sunflower a place to make a
statement. I kept coming up blank, and the more I
kept looking for the round hole, all I kept finding was
the proverbial square peg.

Then, out of nowhere, an email pops up in my inbox. It was from a vendor of both a graphic design-related industry magazine and their annual catalog. The subject line: Call for Art Entry—a contest, this was an opportunity to be featured in their next monthly magazine. The call was for photography, digital designs, paintings, etc. The prompt or topic for the piece to submit was *HOT*.

Well, that just made my heart start pounding at the thought of submitting my photo of the sunflower growing out of the ashes. The ashes were literally created by something as *HOT* as you could get, right? Yes! I'm now talking to myself while reading the submission guidelines and before days' end, my entry is on its way back to them in an email with the photo attachment. The subject line: "After the Fires." That's what I named my photo art piece. If I could only type the sound of the email being sent, you know the sound I'm talking about. Something of a whoosh!

If memory serves, about a month later I received news that my submission, "After the Fires" had won. And even better, it had made it into their annual catalog; a tab page with my image printed full-color, edge-to-edge on one side and the other, my bio, and a full-story description of "After the Fires." I was officially published! What??? Additionally, the publisher sent me 1,000 postcard-sized prints of my image complete with my copyright information. ©Lori Brookes 2019.

What comes next is simply divine intervention; the Universe working to conspire with me or in this case, for me. This was not my plan, I was just trying to make 'something' of my something-something, and the square peg finally dropped in. But wait! This is not the end of the story. A gallery owner in Phoenix, AZ has a copy of the catalog in his hands, sees my tab page, reaches out, and asks if I would be interested in showing my work at his gallery for the city's First Friday Art Event. Gulp. Pause. My work? What work? Up until this point, my passion for photography was merely a hobby, my only intention was to paint from my photos, not to hang them in a gallery or sell them.

I asked him a few questions about the event and his gallery. I told him I would think about it and get back to him. He said I could be part of the last one for the season coming up in June, and it was now May, or I could procrastinate (my word), and join in after the summer when the event starts up again in September. This was one of those forks in the road, a holy shit moment, fear rising on many fronts, and also excitement about something new. Fear and excitement sometimes can feel the same. This moment was a true mix of those two emotions.

Contrary to my norm of staving something off, I jumped in and said, "Yes" to the event, and "Yes" to June. I had less than four weeks to select 12 to 15 pieces of 'my work' and get them professionally printed, matted, mounted, framed, and priced. And since I'm a writer-type and an admitted overachiever, I decided to write something about every one of my kids. That's exactly what they felt like the day I drove to Phoenix to show my work—my kids.

I loved the gallery and the room I had all to myself and the kids. It was perfect, and it was so me. The room's walls were vintage lath and plaster, sans the plaster, and all of the kids were dressed to the nines in their custom frames that looked amazing against the roughed-up wood. I was wearing my best 'I'm an artist' outfit, a black with white polka dots flirty skirt and handmade shoes I had bought in Paris a few years back.

As soon as the kids were installed, I walked outside, feeling a bit queasy in the stomach. My heart and soul were hanging, displayed for anyone to see and read. It was a 10 on my vulnerability chart. This was a first for me to put myself out there—publicly. How I see the world, and what I have to say with my writing. Before now, only for my eyes. My eldest son Randy, who came with me, ran outside and excitedly said, "Mom, you have to get back in here, people are talking about buying some of your pieces." Really? I came back in and sure enough, they were. What struck a chord in my heart was watching people reading the words I had written about my kids, and my work hanging naked on the wall. I sold five of them that night. Oddly I was the only artist to sell anything in the gallery that night. More divinity at work.

I came back home after that weekend in Phoenix, proclaimed myself a photographer, created a website, hung my virtual shingle and that was the beginning of a brand-new chapter in my life. A rebirth of sorts. I went on to create a career around both photography and writing.

What I haven't mentioned is that the chapter before this one was full of epic losses, and the grief that goes along with those losses, my personal and devastating fires. The burning down of a loved life. It turns out, just like the charred trees of the forest, the destruction and devastation of the land, that solitary sunflower grew boldly despite everything. That sunflower that I had tried so desperately to give meaning away to somewhere else, to someone else, was meant for me all along—After the Fires.

LINKED
Christie Walker Bos

I pulled my ponytail through the hole in my baseball cap. My puffy jacket wrapped around me like bubble wrap to ward off the autumn chill.

Hand on the doorknob, ready to make my escape, I shouted to Mom, "I'm going outside."

I had one foot out the door when Mom yelled from the kitchen. "Take your brother."

Not now. "Arghhhh. He doesn't want to go," I argued, the darkness beckoning me like a best friend.

"Yes, I do," the Imp contradicted from his seated position halfway up the stairs.

Three years younger, the Imp, as I called him, was an unwanted shadow that I couldn't shake. He wasn't interested in the stars. Bugs and dinosaurs were his thing. He certainly wouldn't like standing quietly in the cold night to stare into space. He just wanted to be with me … all the time.

The night sky, and its darkness, belonged to me. I didn't want to share it. The Imp would shatter the perfect silence with an endless string of questions that can only come from the mind of a seven-year-old.

"See." Mom came out of the kitchen, drying her hands on a dishtowel. "He wants to go. Scottie, put on your jacket and gloves. I'm going upstairs to shower."

I checked the time on my phone. Only twenty minutes before *they* appear. "Come on, come onnnn," I groaned as I watched my brother spin around and around trying to stuff his other arm into his jacket.

Reluctantly, I helped him, bending down to zip up the front, knowing that the zipping process would have taken precious minutes.

"Let's go," I said and stepped outside.

"What about my gloves?"

I grabbed his hand and pulled him outside. "I'll put them on when we get there."

"Where's there?"

The questions began and I knew there'd be more if I didn't figure out a way to keep him quiet. I had an idea. "Shhh. They'll hear us," I said in a whisper.

"Who will hear us?" Scottie whispered back.

I turned to face him, opening my eyes wide as if I was scared. "The aliens, of course."

"Aliens? Are they the green ones or the gray ones? Are we going to see them or just their spaceships?" Scottie asked, not sounding afraid at all.

Darn. Scaring him into silence hadn't worked. It only created more questions. And how did he know about green and gray aliens? "I don't know. But I do know that if you keep talking, we won't see anything at all. Now come on."

We speed-walked down the street past the glow of our neighbors' houses in search of darkness. At the end of the block, the street dead-ended, and the forest began. We followed a dirt path between sage and rabbit brush that wound its way between groups of pine trees standing as sentinels in the night.

The dirt crunched under our tennis shoes, as we left the neighborhood behind. A coyote yip punctured the silence and Scottie grabbed my hand. His fingers were like little popsicles. I stopped and helped him with his gloves.

"We need to get past these trees for a clear view of the sky and we need to hurry. There's a meadow up ahead with an outcropping of rock. I scouted it out yesterday. It should work. Hold my hand so you don't fall."

Running side-by-side, Scottie had no problem keeping up with me. His legs might be smaller, but he moved them twice as fast. Finally, past the trees, we stepped into a meadow with knee-high grasses and the moonless sky opened before us.

In L.A., light pollution masks all but the brightest stars and planets. At first, when we moved from Pasadena to Big Bear, I was bummed. Leaving all my friends behind, starting over at a new school, living in a smaller house … I couldn't think of one thing I liked about my new home until I walked outside one night. There, arching over our house, glowed the shadowy form of the Milky Way, which I thought were soft clouds until I looked through a pair of binoculars. Then bam! Stars, stars, and more stars.

Up here in the mountains, I could make out dozens of constellations, not just the Big Dipper, like down below. Orion, the hunter, and this three-star belt. Cassiopeia's five-star "W" and the eight stars that create the Teapot. Looking at the Teapot, spouting steam (the misty stars that make the Milky Way look milky) points you in the direction of a massive black hole sitting at the heart of the galaxy, silently gobbling up stars like the Cookie Monster gobbles up cookies.

I oriented myself using the Big Dipper and the North Star. "We need to climb those rocks. Can you do that?"

In answer to my question, Scottie sprinted ahead and started climbing. He made it to the top faster than a lizard. A strange feeling ... admiration, envy ... for my brother? I shook it off and began to climb.

Seated side-by-side, we faced the gray mass to the north which is Gold Mountain. "Look up that way. They should be showing up any minute now."

"How do *you* know? Did the aliens send you a message?"

"I have an app that tells me when and where they'll appear. Now be quiet and keep looking."

For one glorious minute, we sat silently under the night sky. The bright light of Venus had captured my attention when the Imp shouted, "There!"

Appearing one at a time, as if coming out of hyperspace, a bright light floated across the sky at a steady pace, followed by another, then another, then another. They appeared as a train of lights, brighter than the stars, but no match for Venus' brilliance.

"Wow. Where are they going?"

"Shhh. They'll hear you. Just watch. Let's see how many there are."

As we counted, more and more lights popped into existence, twenty-one in total, before the first light in the train disappeared. Each light blinked out in the same spot as the first, until they were all gone.

The Imp exploded like a supernova. "Where'd they go? Are they coming back? Do you think they are going to land or keep on flying? Should we tell Mom? Did you take a picture? A movie? No one is going to believe us."

"Let's go," I said. "I'll answer your questions on the walk back."

Safely back on flat ground, I rattled off the answers to his questions as we walked. "They're circling the earth. They'll be back tomorrow night. They're not going to land, and sure, you can tell Mom. I didn't take a picture or a movie, but I will tomorrow."

"Tomorrow? Can we come again? Can *I* come again?"

"Sure," I said with a smile he couldn't see.

On the way home, the Imp bombarded me with nonstop questions about aliens and the stars. Since astronomy was *my* thing, for once I enjoyed answering and explaining. I didn't tell him the "alien spaceships" were Starlink satellites.

When I opened the front door, Scottie released his pent-up energy, sending him up the stairs two at a time. I followed him and headed to my room. Even with my door closed, I could still hear my brother's excited voice as he described what he saw to Mom.

* * *

High School already was a treacherous place, filled with pitfalls, missteps, and unknown disasters around every corner, without throwing in the added stress of a freshman brother stalking you, ready to shout a cheery, "Hi, Kimberly," when you least expected it. I had managed to walk the tightrope between "with it" and "clueless" up until the start of my senior year. Then three years of a carefully calculated life came crashing down when Scottie showed up.

Of course, Mom wanted me to drive him to school. Sure. But bringing him home? That presented a problem. I stayed after school on Monday, Tuesday, and Wednesday participating in club activities. Lucky for me, you had to be a sophomore before you could participate in the Robotics or Programming clubs, which left Scottie sitting outside the classroom playing games on his phone. But the Astronomy club accepted everyone, even freakish little brothers who wanted to sit next to you at every meeting. There were other freshmen in the club and eventually, Scottie had nerdy friends of his own.

The Christmas of my senior year, Scottie and I shouted with the same joy as we unwrapped twin telescopes. Donning jackets and gloves like we did years ago to watch the aliens, we headed outside, stomping through the snow, to set up our telescopes. Using the fourth star in the Cassiopeia "W" I zeroed in on the spiral Andromeda Galaxy, the nearest major galaxy to the Milky Way. On a clear night, with the naked eye, Andromeda appears as a fuzzy star. But with my new telescope, the true beauty of the galaxy came into focus.

"Wow," I said to Scottie, who was still fiddling with the knobs on his scope.

"What do you have?"

"The Andromeda Galaxy. What were you trying to find?" I asked, as Scottie and I switched places.

"The Pleiades. Wow is right. Look at all those stars," he said, with his eye pressed against the rubber cup.

While he was oohing and ahhing, I found the star cluster called the Seven Sisters. Turning the focus knob, the stars pop into focus. "I have the Pleiades if you want to come look."

Scottie and I switched places again. "There're more than seven sisters. There must be thousands."

Closer to three thousand, I thought, but who's counting.

* * *

That summer, while I packed clothes, my computer, and school supplies for college, Scottie sulked. He'd be entering sophomore year in the fall and was too cool to cry anymore. But based on how he kept leaving the room anytime Mom, Dad, and I talked about college, I suspected he wanted to.

It wasn't until our final goodbye outside my new dorm room, that Scottie finally broke down, a single tear escaping to run down his cheek. "Who's going to look at the night sky with me?"

I put an arm around his shoulder, and with Mom and Dad walking ahead, led Scottie down the hall to the exit. "You have the Astronomy club."

"Not the same," he said stubbornly. "They only meet once a month. We used to go outside almost every night. It just won't be the same without you."

"I'll be back before you know it at Christmas. The winter sky is the best, anyway."

"I know," he pouted.

I knew he was going to miss me, but was too cool to say so, so I did. "I'm going to miss you, you big Imp," I said, squeezing his shoulder in a half hug.

Scottie sniffed but didn't say a word.

* * *

Over the years, the night sky kept Scottie and me close. Even though we were seldom in the same place at the same time, Scottie in college on the East Coast, and me working in Pasadena at the Jet Propulsion Lab, we could still enjoy celestial events together.

Mom and Dad had downsized their house in Big Bear to a cozy cabin with one guest room with bunk beds, and a hot tub for their "aching bones." In that hot tub, Scottie and I witnessed the best meteor shower of my life, and I'd seen dozens.

We'd arrived in Big Bear the week before Thanksgiving in time to catch the Leonid Meteor shower under a clear mountain sky. The peak viewing hours were from 2 to 4 a.m. After a home-cooked meal and free-flowing wine, Scottie and I climbed into the narrow bunk beds, each setting alarms for 2 a.m., determined not to miss the event.

Four hours later, towels draped across our shoulders, dressed in bathing suits and sandals with ski beanies on our heads, we left the warmth of the cabin for 104-degree water. Steam rose into the crisp night air as we removed the spa cover and climbed in, involuntary ahhhs escaping our frozen lips. Using our towels as pillows on the edge of the spa, we tilted our heads back in unison and stared into the velvet night.

"How long do you think we'll have to wait," asked Scottie. Before I could answer, a flash of light streaked across the dark blanket of the night sky. "Did you see it?"

"Yes. That was a good one. Oh. Did you see that one?" he pointed.

"I missed it. There," I said, but the streak disappeared before I could point.

"I saw it. Seems like this is going to be a good one. Maybe we should count how many we see."

"I've seen three," I said.

"Four … and five," we shrieked in unison.

An hour and a half later, our fingers and toes looking like prunes, Scottie and I called it quits when we reached 300 meteors.

Never before or since, have I seen so many meteors in one night.

* * *

The phone call I'll never forget woke me at three in the morning. "There's been an accident."

As I pulled on jeans and a sweatshirt, my mind screamed, "No, no, no. Not Scottie."

Luckily, traffic was light as I drove like a shooting star from Pasadena to Orange County, where Scottie now lived after graduating from college. Gripping the steering wheel like I wanted to strangle it, my mind replayed favorite moments with my brother bringing on a river of tears, making the oncoming lights glow like spiral galaxies. Not until my phone announced, "You've arrived at your destination," did I snap out of the trance I'd been in to find myself in front of the hospital.

Hours dripped by, like the IV in his arm, as I sat holding Scottie's hand. My parents stood like shadows in the corner of the room, my mother's sobbing creating the soundtrack of the moment.

I remembered the night in Big Bear when Scottie and I looked up together and found a common interest that cemented a friendship that spanned the years. No matter where we were, we could cast our eyes skyward and feel connected, forever linked by the night sky.

I leaned forward to catch Scottie's whispered words.

"Remember the night we saw the aliens?"

I nodded and squeezed his hand.

"That was the best night ever, right?"

"Right. And the night of the 300 meteors."

"Yes. 300." His words floated away, evaporating like lake mist disappearing with the warmth of the rising sun.

A sigh as soft as the flap of a butterfly's wing escaped his lips before my brother took flight, free to dance among the stars.

REMINISCE
Yvonne Phillips

Ahh, holidays in the mountains, nothing quite compares. In my opinion, not even the Alps. If memory serves, the winter I spent in Europe was cold and rainy … that's when I met Rainer. I'd just turned a significant age, and my long-term relationship had ended because of a younger woman. It was a bad time for me. Rainer was twenty-four and a pleasant diversion despite me breaking my leg.

He'd said skiing was easy—easy, my ass. I had to curtail part of my tour to allow myself to heal. The doctor said exhaustion from working too much had led to my accident and that I needed lots of bed rest.

Sometimes, I can still recall the room at the inn where I recuperated. Tall windows afforded me a view of gently falling snow. The glow from the fireplace cast warmth and a feeling of tranquility while I lay snuggled under an eiderdown comforter. Rainer stayed with me most of the time. Cuddling, whispering sweet nothings, apologizing endlessly, and massaging my body. He said it was to keep up my circulation and encourage a speedy recovery. Perhaps, but I still remember his soothing hands. And thinking of him still brings a smile.

Now, I sit in my hilltop home on the Fawnskin side of the lake—the side with the best views. From my little nest, I can see everything Big Bear Valley offers without all the hustle, bustle, and traffic.

In the summer, my view is of the lake and the boaters. Not to mention the jet skis, sailboats, kayaks, canoes, paddle boards, and swimmers. People fish from bobbing boats and the shoreline. Throughout the year, the lights from the village across the lake shine into the darkness, reminding me that I am not alone in this mountain valley.

The Fourth of July brings many visitors to our side of the lake. The view of the fireworks is splendid, and the hundreds, if not thousands, of car headlights when they head home reminds me of how many enjoy our yearly display.

Autumn brings the smell of wood smoke and the wisps of it ascending from fireplaces spread throughout the valley. Our oaks normally have green leaves; they turn yellow at the first hint of fall and put on a fine show, turning to gold and then copper as the weather grows colder. Interspaced with the golden oaks and evergreen of the pines are the bright orange and red leaves of the various maples.

Along with brilliant fall colors, cold nights, blazing fireplaces, and wood smoke come memories. Poignant times and happy times are embedded in these walls. And, in the silence of the dark, lonely nights, they reach out to me.

Memories of friends and family, some nearby, and some afar. Some we only now know because of their holiday cards.

Scrolling through Facebook, I check my friends list. There are some listed that I don't recognize. Who are they? How did they get there? But I know most of the others and happily push the LIKE button by their stories and pictures. Then, mixed in with plans for an upcoming excursion or event comes a jolt of the unexpected. Pictures of friends who are no longer with us smile back at me from these digital pages. I pause to push down the pain in my heart and remember something pleasant about them, an outing or a happy time and place, a kind word, or a gentle touch. It wrenches my heart that I can no longer send them a joke or a funny story. Sadly, they are no longer just a phone call away.

My thoughts run further back in time to before I was grown. I forget how old I was the year we had a giant Christmas tree that almost touched the ceiling. Presents surrounded it because Christmas was growing near. My mother helped me mark the days off on a calendar.

A grand piano sat in the corner of our large living room. On the opposite corner stood a large brick fireplace where Santa would come down the chimney and fill my stocking.

With Daddy being a stuntman and Mommy singing radio jingles, they had many friends in what they called the "industry." My folks hosted many parties. I remember everyone gathered around the piano, singing and drinking martinis.

One night, close to Christmas, they let me stay up late and sing some Carrols with them. That's when Regina Remington was born.

Henry Jones had a top-rated Big Band. He toured the United States and parts of Europe. They had a group of singers, a single blond lady singer, dancers, a comedian, and a magician. My folks took me to see them once. And after all these years, I still remember. It must have been a great show.

And that night at the Christmas party, Mr. Jones got all excited when he heard me sing. He asked my mom if I could sing in the show they were putting on for the radio audience. She said yes.

The radio station got lots of calls. The public thought I sang better than Shirley Temple and almost better than Deanna Durbin. The movie offers rolled in. I don't exactly know if the audiences were tired of kid movies, Shirley Temple, Margaret O'Brien, and The Little Rascals, or if my acting was terrible, but the film didn't draw an audience. Maybe it was the writing.

With my career on the wane, it hit rock bottom with my teen years. I think the only ones that escaped with their careers intact were Natalie, Elizabeth, Judy, and Mickey.

But with my advancing teen years came a stronger voice. The music industry was moving away from the Big Band sound, and I loved the new freedom it gave me.

Appearing on shows like The Milton Berle Show, Red Skelton, Ed Sullivan, and Andy Williams gave me back my self-confidence. There were many more, but they all went by in a blur.

Then came Elvis, along with sex, drugs, and rock and roll—life changes. People change, and social mores are ever-changing. What was decent and correct in one decade is not always so in the following decades.

Being in the entertainment industry put me on the leading edge of change. And I'll admit that at twenty-one I wore the shortest mini-skirts and highest boots I could find. I went to the wildest parties, drank too much, and smoked too much pot. But when they brought out the white powder and the pills, my tamer self took over.

That's when I met Robert Thomas. Bobby was in the business by way of being a record producer. Yes, he attended those pot-smoke-filled parties, but he didn't do drugs, not even pot, and stuck to his rule of only having one drink a night. No matter how long that night proved to be.

We met at an after-party. I was holding a match to light a joint when his hand closed around my wrist. He blew out the flame and kissed my palm. "Why don't you get high on life instead of that?" He nodded toward the unlit doobie in my other hand.

His approach, out of the norm for sure, captured my interest. We left the party and went for coffee. Yes, coffee at one in the morning. We dated for two months before we got married.

To escape the hectic music life and Hollywood whirl, we bought a tiny one-room cabin perched on the side of a mountain. It even had an outhouse. We'd drive up the mountain every Friday night and come home late on Sunday. We loved Big Bear. Finally, we gave in to our friends and families wanting to visit and added three small but big enough bedrooms and two bathrooms.

Bobby drew up the plans, and we did most of the work ourselves. Working on the cabin every weekend and ten days in the summer was a labor of love. And the cabin glowed that love from its new walls.

Bobby died ten years from the day we got the permit finalized. He'd flown to Detroit on business. The plane and the other 162 people it carried crashed during a massive thunderstorm over Kansas.

After his funeral, I continued to come up every Friday. It gave me peace, and I always felt a part of him there. In time, my visits slowed a bit. I still sang at small venues and private clubs. And after five or so years of being alone, friends introduced me to Charles. He hated the mountains and got carsick driving to the cabin. So, in time, I too, quit coming. I almost sold it several times, but something inside me said no.

A few years later, Charles dumped me for a newer model. That's when I met Rainer. He's coming to California on business soon and wants to get together.

I invited him to the cabin. I'm even older now, but then again, so is he. We'll have to wait and see what happens.

SNAKES I HAVE KNOWN AND LOVED

Karene Horst

My fingers clenched the brake levers as I skidded my mountain bike to a halt. A rattlesnake blocked the Woodland Trail. Its thick body extended perpendicular to my front tire. I'd managed to stop a safe distance ten feet away. Glad I had my eyes glued to the terrain ahead of my bike instead of gazing at the granite boulders, evergreens, red pine-needle beardtongue and other wildflowers that create a mesmerizing trailside backsplash.

I straddled my bike, planting my feet on the ground, and watched the snake inch its way across my path. From its viper head to the tip of its impressive set of rattles, the snake measured at least four feet in length. Not in any hurry, this guy knew who had the right of way. The snake had raised its rattles, pointing skyward but silent to protect them while traversing the rough ground. I stood still as I admired the undulating geometric patterns of stripes and triangles. Fantastic!

For the past ten years I've mountain biked and hiked all over this portion of the San Bernardino Mountains, and this was only my second rendezvous with a rattlesnake in Big Bear.

The first time biking the same trail, I came upon a tourist poking a stick at a baby rattlesnake cowering next to a rock. I wanted to say something but decided against interfering, as I resort to conflict-avoidance regarding men as well as rattlesnakes. Pedaling past, I prayed both stupid human and wild critter would survive the experience unharmed.

I have learned to respect and cherish these amazing creatures and their vital place in our ecosystem. But I have to confess I have not always demonstrated a positive attitude let alone love for snakes, rattlers and otherwise.

My childhood amidst the manicured suburbs of Santa Monica, California, limited any contact with snakes outdoors. Occasionally one of my brothers would capture a tiny garter snake in our backyard. Sad to say, I don't believe many of these prisoners survived.

Brother Jim kept pythons as pets. He had a friendly Burmese Python he would drape around his arms and shoulders as he strutted through the house shirtless. Once he had me "babysit" the snake. "Don't make any sudden movements," Jim warned me. "He doesn't like that." I cringed as the python tightened its clasp on my forearm while its head edged toward my neck to hide in my hair. I grew accustomed to walking into the bathroom and seeing a python swimming in the bathtub. Once a snake escaped from its enclosure, and after several weeks my poor mother found it curled up behind a bed she was making.

I did not join the neighborhood gang to watch the python feeding on live mice. But tame pythons and garden-variety snakes never really bothered me–they don't have venom-filled fangs. Other than sidewinders or various species of the deadly fer-de-lance behind glass at a zoo herpetarium, I'd never met a snake that I feared could hurt me.

Then I moved to rural Missouri and chanced upon my first wild snake. It was a nonvenomous black snake that had somehow managed to sneak its way into my kitchen. When I saw it dive from the counter back into its hiding place, I screamed. I ran out of the house, called my then-husband, and demanded he leave work immediately to return home and protect me from this horrible creature. Kill it!

He laughed at me. Nope. We don't kill black snakes, even those who manage to slip inside the house. That black snake had probably eaten some of the mice that sprinkled poop throughout my cupboards. He told me I had nothing to worry about from the harmless reptile. I can't remember how long it took me to venture back inside my home.

He did believe in killing copperheads, however, as they had a nasty, venomous bite. He would shoot them with a rifle whenever he discovered one lounging under an overturned canoe next to our lake or slithering through the woodpile. One time a copperhead bit him in the leg while he mowed the yard. He hated them.

I grew to hate them too and joined the battle. After finding a copperhead sunning itself near our backdoor, I used a shovel to cut it in half while I perched on top of our four-wheeler to avoid its fangs.

It seems I practically tripped over copperheads everywhere on our farm! They usually escaped my wrath by writhing into a pile of rocks or under a bush while I flailed away at them with my shovel or some other metal garden implement.

Then a different type of snake strayed into the yard of my Ozark home. My Labrador barked in unleashed fury while the snake hissed and opened its mouth as if to bite, its head and neck spreading wide like a cobra's. I yelled at my dog as the snake lunged toward him. Its markings reminded me of a rattlesnake, but I was no expert. I grabbed my shovel and cut off its head before it could strike. A friend who worked for the state conservation department practically took off mine.

"That was a hognose snake! They are so cool! They're not venomous. They usually don't even bite. They just puff up their jaws and act aggressive as a defensive measure!" He shook his head at me in disgust.

Here I thought I was protecting my dog, and instead, I killed an innocent being. Shame swamped me. This run-in started a gradual opening of my heart to snakes, whether deadly or not. I watched nature programs with my kids, marveling with them at these magnificent and beautiful animals. I gained an appreciation for their place in our world and a respect for their contribution toward making this a healthy planet, such as controlling the rodent population. I finally accepted their right to exist–and my responsibility to coexist.

Ten years ago I had my first wild rattlesnake sighting on a foggy spring day hiking at Montana de Oro State Park on California's central coast. The rattlesnake gave up on finding a warm, quiet spot in the middle of the dirt path and slowly glided into the sagebrush while my friend and I stood a respectful distance away. WOW!

I'm surprised I did not get bit the next time I crossed a rattlesnake. During an evening stroll on the paved streets of an Arizona neighborhood, my companion suddenly stopped walking and turned to me.

"I think I just stepped on a snake!"

We swung around and her flashlight illuminated a baby rattlesnake. Its small triangular head was pointed in the direction I had been walking, right next to my friend. The snake's head would have been inches from my sandaled foot.

The stunned snake froze in a straight line as we gingerly backed away. A neighbor cautiously scooped the snake into a deep bucket and promised to relocate it to a new home in an area uninhabited by people. Only then did we hear the buzzing sound from its rattles, as the young snake angrily lunged up at our faces peering over the rim from high above.

One sunny summer day a few years ago, my daughter and I hiked through the woods to splash around in Deep Creek off the Pacific Crest Trail. We found an empty sand beach just past a large boulder beyond the crowd of swimmers and sun worshippers next to Aztec Falls. We spread our towels close to the water's edge and stretched out on our backsides, resting on our elbows and gabbing while savoring the view. Not five minutes later, my daughter looked past me and shrieked.

"There's a snake!" Instinctively we both jumped to our feet and headed in the opposite direction.

The adult Southern Pacific rattlesnake had slid from beneath a bush that we just walked by and crept four feet toward us before turning back to the underbrush. I could tell by the bend in its body that when outstretched, its fangs had hovered within less than two feet of me–striking distance. I thought we announced our presence by making enough noise splashing through the river, talking, and pacing around to locate the perfect place to lay our towels on the sand. Fortunately, once the rattler realized its mistake, it socially distanced itself before I made a sudden movement and forced the snake to go on the defensive.

I shuddered. I've stumbled across snakes before, but this time a dangerous one approached me. These rattlesnake encounters have made me increasingly wary of moving about in the outdoors. I've educated myself as much as possible about rattlesnakes so I can overcome my rising fear whenever I wander.

I wear ankle-high boots while hiking of course, but I've considered protective gators up to my knees for both hiking and mountain biking. Experts recommend loose pant legs and thick denim jeans to diminish the severity of a venomous snake bite.

Researchers also emphasize vigilance to avoid rattlesnakes. I no longer walk outside my home next to the San Bernardino National Forest without staring at the ground in search of a leaf-and-dirt-colored body spiraled against my deck or a trash bin. I used to wear flip flops while roaming in my backyard. Now I wear boots that protect me well past my ankles.

Basically I watch where I step or where I put my hands. I only let my guard down when frost or snow steers rattlers underground.

Rattlesnakes rove underfoot any time of the year, depending on the temperature. When the mercury drops, rattlesnakes gather and establish dens in burrows or in rocky crevices that retain heat. When it's really cold, snakes go into winter brumation, a state of dormancy with brief periods of activity. In mild weather rattlesnakes will sunbathe on a rock outcropping or a trail.

As temperatures rise, rattlesnakes avoid the harshest time of day in the sun to keep from overheating by finding shady places in thick stands of grass or brush, under logs or rocks. Beneath homes, decks and sheds.

During spring and summer, rattlesnakes travel outside more in the morning, at dusk, and into the night.

Most rattlesnake bites occur from April through October when the weather encourages both people and rattlesnakes to cross paths.

Human aggression or inattention cause most rattlesnake bites: trying to agitate or capture the animal; sticking a hand into a rock crevice; walking through thick grass or brushy areas; forgetting to check rocks, stumps or logs before sitting on or stepping over them. Rattlesnakes can swim and sometimes are found in lakes and streams.

Rattlesnakes are not vicious. They avoid people and retreat when possible if given the space to escape. Snakes hunt in stealth, trying to stay incognito until a mouse or a ground squirrel scampers by. They also remain motionless and silent so as not to advertise their presence to potential predators, such as birds of prey and coyotes. When a rattlesnake perceives danger, its first reaction is to freeze, relying on its camouflage to hide. Unfortunately, their survival techniques make them easier for humans to blunder into.

When startled or provoked, they may rattle a warning, but not always before striking.

Once the rattler decides to issue its ominous alarm to an intruder, it starts with a slow frequency shake. Ch-ch-ch. A sound similar to that of an irrigation sprinkler just starting up. As a rattler feels more threatened, the frequency of the rattle increases to a steady buzzing sound. Just listening to these sounds on the internet makes my skin crawl.

Rattlesnakes do not need to coil up in order to strike and bite, but they bank on this grand posture as a defensive measure that makes them appear larger, more menacing, and when they sense wriggling away would make them more vulnerable to attack.

Striking and biting consumes energy and venom they need to kill and digest food, so rattlesnakes restrain themselves as much as possible. Even when they sink their fangs into flesh, approximately twenty-five percent of the time they deliver a "dry bite"–they don't inject venom.

If you or a companion are ever bit, remain calm to slow the spread of the venom. Remove anything that could constrict swelling, such as clothing, shoes, watches or jewelry. Immediately contact emergency medical personnel and transport the victim to an emergency room as soon as possible. Don't apply a tourniquet or ice, avoid any medications, and never cut the wound or try to suck out the venom. If the bite is on an extremity, elevate the limb if possible but keep below victim's heart.

Decades ago, my Aunt Martha was bitten in the finger by a rattlesnake while weeding her garden in Mandeville Canyon. Her husband rushed her to the emergency room. Her hand and arm swelled up and her face went numb. Once she received the antivenom treatment and the swelling subsided, she needed morphine to control the pain. The hospital kept her overnight for observation. Today, she can't even tell you which finger got nipped.

Along with my family history of surviving rattlesnake bites, I find comfort from the statistics. Every year approximately 7,000 to 8,000 venomous snake bites in the US result in only five deaths.

Then there's the US Centers for Disease Control and Prevention's 2014 report that humans face a greater risk of dying from falling off a ladder or getting hit by lightning than from a rattlesnake bite.

Our local hospital, Bear Valley Community Healthcare District, reports treating only two rattlesnake bites to humans during the past three years.

Dogs present a unique challenge when it comes to rattlesnakes. Keep your fur baby on a leash and on the trail and prevent them from sniffing under shrubs and brush. Some dogs learn to keep a safe distance through Rattlesnake Aversion Training. Vaccinating your dog or cat for rattlesnake bites can lessen the severity, but any rattlesnake bite still requires medical attention. Each year approximately 300,000 pets, including cats, are bitten by venomous snakes throughout the US, resulting in a five percent death rate.

* * *

My third and last meetup with a rattlesnake took place on an early June day while biking on my favorite local trail, The Woodland. A mild, nontechnical ride I can cruise alone when my biking buddies are too busy to join. The Woodland Trail is so popular with hikers that I know if I have a mishap, someone will ramble by soon afterward, notice my prone body splayed haphazardly into a buckthorn bush, and call for help. I usually do at least three laps with a cool down ride on the paved Alpine Pedal Path next to the lake.

And as usual, my eyes scoured the trail ahead of me for snakes. I saw what I took for a slim, straight tree limb less than a foot long lying on the trail perpendicular to my front tire. Just as I rode over it I realized my mistake. A snake.

I doubled back and confirmed that I'd just wheeled over a baby Southern Pacific rattlesnake. Now, its body kinked slightly into a wavy S curve as it slowly inched across the trail and found refuge under a log beside the path.

Had my tires rolling onto the snake's spine hurt it in any way? I felt awful. I remained a good distance away, maybe five feet, as I watched the young rattler coil into a circle, its black eyes glaring as it repeatedly stuck out its forked tongue at me. No warning rattle. The snake appeared undamaged. I apologized and promised I'd be more careful next time I saw what looked like a lifeless branch in my path.

I suggest you do the same.

58

THE NUMAN IN THE YARD
Christie Walker Bos

Standing next to the trash can at the post office, Don flipped through his stack of mail, mentally sorting as he went … junk, trash, junk, interesting, bill, bill, what the hell? The white envelope stamped with "Violation" in capital red letters made Don sigh. "Not again."

Twenty minutes later, he slapped the offending letter on the kitchen table in front of his wife, Barbara. Now it was Barbara's turn to sigh, shaking her head, making her long gray braid swing across her back like a pendulum. "Oh, no. Here we go again. Should I call or do you want to?"

"I'll do it," Don said as he ripped open the envelope and read the weed abatement notice. "Same thing every year. The Numan will not be pleased."

* * *

Don walked around his yard, hands stuffed in the pockets of his blue jeans, as he mumbled under his breath. His boots crunched the gravel of the pathway as he made his way between a pair of Serviceberry shrubs that had grown as large as trees. "They are going to tell me to remove most of these branches. The Numan isn't going to like it."

Stepping carefully around and over any new growth, Don said hello to emerging native plants, the hardy survivors who'd spent the winter buried under two feet of snow. "Don't worry. The Numan and I will protect you. I'm not going to whack you down just as you're getting started. That's no way to treat something so special. Right?" He paused to listen as if someone or something was going to answer him.

Don nodded to the breeze that made the new oak leaves dance. "That's what I thought."

He continued his walk around his yard which sat on a third of an acre, bordering the San Bernardino National Forest. The caw caw of a raven beckoned his eyes to the sky. Dozens of towering Jeffrey Pines cut the sky into a patchwork quilt of blue allowing only a momentary look of the black-winged beauty. Don cawed to the raven, laughing when it answered him. Continuing his walk, he paused when he spotted a turf of Cheatgrass, hiding amongst a group of poppy plants. Bending over, he pulled the offensive invasive species and left it on the path to be retrieved later.

For over 30 years, Don and Barbara had nurtured their yard, collecting, and spreading native seed in the fall and hand weeding in the Spring and Summer, often on their hands and knees. Invasive species, if left unchecked, would overtake and smother the natives. No Roundup or weedwhackers are allowed in this yard. After years of diligent care, plants flourished, birds nested and sang, squirrels and chipmunks frolicked, and the occasional hawk dined, all under the watchful eye of The Numan.

Standing straight, Don noted the time on his watch. "Government people. Almost as bad as the cable guy."

Taking a seat on a log bench, Don took a moment to survey his yard, nodding his approval at each area—bird central, as Barbara called it, with the bird feeders and a bird bath, the wooden bat boxes attached high on the pines to give the bats a place to roost, the edible plant beds with the delicious dandelions they would add to their salads all spring and summer, the wood pile with its hidden nooks for mice and the occasional hungry snake, and The Numan's favorite spot, the prickly patch.

The prickly patch sat in the corner of the yard furthest away from the house. The area played host to thorny wild roses with their soft pink flowers that did a great job of hiding the chain-linked fence. In addition to the wild roses, the spiny Prickly Poppies—whose large white tissue paper thin flowers would take center stage starting in early summer—and a single Mojave Mound cactus—who was preparing to wow everyone with its red, trumpet-shaped flowers, the cactus' moment of glory—added more prickles to the prickly patch.

Next to the bench grew one of Don's favorite native plant, the aromatic rose sage. Too early in the season for its deep pink flowers, the plant's leaves were a delight as the soft blue/green stood out amongst the darker shades of the other nearby plants. He reached down and rubbed a leaf between his thumb and fingers. Bringing his fingertips to his nose, he inhaled the strong sage scent. The aroma's calming effect transported him to a mellow state that evaporated with the sound of a large vehicle tearing up the long gravel driveway sending small white rocks flying in every direction.

Shaking his head, he pushed himself off the bench and went to meet the inspector. Turns out there were two inspectors, a tall, older man with thin balding hair that Don recognized, and a mid-sized youngish woman with bright blond hair pulled high into a ponytail. By the time Don walked across the yard, the woman stood rigid next to the car clutching a clipboard to her chest.

Newbie, he thought as he approached.

"Hey Don," said the male inspector, his voice already sounding tired and resigned.

"Hey, Carl," Don answered and stepped up to shake his hand. "So, we're doing *this* again?"

"Yep. Rules are rules."

"But are they really, Carl? Rules are made by people, and as we know, people are flawed. That's what The Numan says, and I tend to agree with him."

"The Numan?" the young inspector asked.

"Yes. Only a few lucky people ever get to meet him in all his glory. I'm one of those people." Don looked her up and down, pulling at his gray and white beard thoughtfully. "I'm guessing you aren't very lucky, are you?"

The young woman stood straighter, shoulders back, chin out. "I wouldn't say that. I'm as lucky as the next person. Why the other day, I won five dollars on a Scratcher."

Carl shook his head slightly. "Don, be nice. This is Kimberly Johnson. She joined our team this year and I'm showing her the ropes."

Don forced a smile. "Ms. Johnson. Follow me and I'll give you the standard tour."

Kimberly cocked her head in confusion. "We're not here for a tour. Your yard violates several ordinances. We are here upon your request to explain to YOU what has to be done to bring you into compliance."

"Let me guess," Don said, looking at her clipboard. "You think I have weeds that need to be whacked, debris that must be removed, and branches that need trimming. I assure you that is not the case. Everything here in my yard is here for a reason and has a purpose. When I've completed my tour, I'm sure you will agree."

Kimberly looked around the yard at what she perceived to be a disarray of wild, untamed plants and snorted. Don looked over her head at Carl and rolled his eyes.

"You can lead the way, Ms. Johnson. Why don't you show me these *weeds* you want me to remove," suggested Don.

"Fine."

Kimberly hadn't walked more than a few feet before she stopped in front of a bed outlined in rocks. "Here. These are weeds, and they need to be removed."

Don shook his head. "Those are dandelions. We harvest their leaves for our salads. Very tasty. Would you like to try one?" He bent down and picked a leaf, then held it out to her.

She turned her head and scrunched up her nose. "No thank you."

Don shrugged and popped the leaf in his mouth. "The leaves taste earthy and bitter, a bit like chicory or endive, but not as sharp as arugula. We mix them with spinach and romaine lettuce, which we also grow in the summer. These plants are food. Nowhere in your code does it say that growing food is a violation, does it?"

Kimberly turned her head and looked at Carl, who shook his head. Turning back to Don, she said, "I guess not."

They walked on, Kimberly leading the way, pointing out *weed* after *weed*, with Don naming each plant, explaining its unique properties, some of them medicinal and others edible. "I'm sure you recognize this little beauty. It's California's state flower, the poppy. Surely you don't expect me to dig up the state flower."

"Of course not. Poppies are fine. What about that mound of discarded wood? It's a fire hazard."

"I believe it's far enough away from the house to make it legal. If you want, we can measure the distance to the house."

Kimberly sighed. "That won't be necessary."

"That wood pile is also home to a couple of mouse families and the occasional snake, which is why I don't disturb the wood all winter."

At the mention of the snake, Kimberly gave the ramshackle wood pile a wider berth. "Let me get this straight. You have a wood pile, but you don't use the wood because it would disturb the mice who live there?"

"The Numan told me to leave the wood alone. Besides, we have a gas heater, so we don't need the wood for our fireplace."

"Who is this Numan fellow you keep talking about?"

Carl dropped his head. "I'm going to sit on the bench and enjoy the view."

Don smiled. Carl had heard the Numan speech several times. He could probably give the speech himself if he were so inclined.

"The Numan isn't a fellow. The Numan just is. Follow me." Don walked towards the back of the yard that butted up against the National Forest boundary. The brush became thicker, and even though she was a foot shorter than Don, Kimberly still had to duck to pass under the branches of two smaller Jeffrey Pines.

"These pines need to be removed. They are smaller than six inches in diameter. You need to thin out all these smaller trees."

Ignoring her, Don stopped before they arrived at the prickly patch. "Do you see over there, just the other side of the fence? That is the forest. If you walk through the forest, you'll see all sizes of trees … grandparents that are hundreds of years old, parents ranging in age from 30 to 90 years old, then the teenagers, like these trees you want me to cut down, 13 to 19 years old, and of course, the wee tikes, the baby trees that are just coming up."

"But the code says, you have to thin your trees out."

"Does the code know which trees are sick with bark beetle or some other illness? What happens when I arbitrarily pick this tree to chop down," Don said, placing a hand on one of the teenagers. "And then it turns out that this guy was the healthy one and the one we left standing dies a year later. When a tree naturally dies … on its own … then and only then do I cut it down. I agree dead trees are a fire hazard and I dutifully remove them. That's how I add to my wood pile."

"But the code says—" Kimberly tried.

"The Numan says this is flawed thinking and I believe it."

Kimberly crossed her arms, the clipboard held protectively to her chest. "Again, who is this Numan fellow?"

"He's not actually a person … more of a spiritual being, a guardian of life, the forest, the earth. He wants mankind to live its best life and quite frankly, he is not pleased with how things have been progressing since the industrial revolution. We're making a mess of the place."

Kimberly rolled her eyes. "Oh. So, he's a nutjob environmentalist who doesn't believe in following the rules."

"I'm not sure he's an environmentalist as he's part of the environment, but you are right about the rules. He doesn't care about them one bit," Don laughed.

"We are a country of rules. Without them, there would be chaos," Kimberly insisted.

"Maybe I should have said, he doesn't care about man-made rules. He absolutely believes in the laws of nature, things like gravity and the circle of life, that sort of stuff."

Kimberly squinted her eyes at Don. "I don't believe you. I think you're making this stuff up. There is no such thing as a Numan."

"Oh, there most certainly is, right Carl?" Don shouted in Carl's direction.

Kimberly turned to see Carl nod. "Okay, then where is this Numan?"

"He's everywhere, especially in the forest." Don pointed to the prickly patch. "Make your way through the wild roses. There is a small path there. Be careful of the thorns and don't step on the prickly poppies or the Mojave Mound."

"The Mojave Mound?"

"The big round cactus. She's getting ready to bloom. There's a break in the fence line. I keep it open for The Numan so he can come and go as he likes. I usually commune with him around those big boulders and that oak tree. That's the best place to experience The Numan."

"This is a joke, right? What is he? Some homeless guy?"

"Far from it. All of this is his home. You don't have to go if you're scared," Don said, with just a hint of a challenge in his voice.

"No. Don't go," Carl called weakly from his position on the bench.

Carl's comment was the final straw. Kimberly stomped off toward the wall of wild roses, walking back and forth until she found the narrow pathway. She turned her head and gave the two old guys a smile that seemed to say, "I'll show you."

Halfway down the path, thorny branches reached out and snagged her pants and the sleeves of her shirt, but she pulled away and pushed on until she cleared the fence and marched up the slight incline toward the lone oak tree and the pile of house-size boulders.

Don walked over and joined Carl on the bench. "Is the wasp nest still in that old oak?" Carl asked.

"I think so. She should be fine if she doesn't disturb them."

Both men turned in unison to the sound of Kimberly's voice. "Come out, come out, wherever you are."

"Oh, that's not good."

"Not good at all," Carl agreed. "You know, one of these days, an inspector who is allergic to wasp stings might get stung. You could get into trouble."

"I don't see how. The wasps are not on my property. Besides, The Numan is the one who riles up the wasps, not me. I'm just sitting here minding my own business."

"That Numan is a problem," Carl sighed. "How long do you think this will take?"

Don turned and listened as Kimberly continued to yell into the forest. "Should be any minute now. The Numan is not very patient with people who aren't respectful."

Then, right on cue, the men heard Kimberly scream. They turned to watch as she ran down the slope, one hand holding her clipboard over her head while the other arm swatted the air frantically. She didn't bother with the opening in Don's fence but veered off to the left to cut across the neighbor's yard with its trimmed hedges and perfectly spaced trees, yelling the entire time.

Carl and Don slowly rose to their feet. "I guess we're going," said Carl, arching his back, then cracking his neck.

"Yep. This is your last year, right?" Don asked.

"Nope."

The two men headed to the car. "I thought you were retiring."

"Me, too, but the wife wants to go on this fancy cruise, so I thought I'd work another year. Save a bit more money."

Don nodded. "Until next year then."

Carl walked around to the driver's side of the car. Kimberly was already seated in the passenger seat, looking straight ahead. Don caught a glimpse of a silvery tear running down her cheek. Poor thing, he thought. I hope she didn't get stung.

Carl opened the car door and paused before climbing inside. "Say hi to The Numan for me," he said over the roof of the car.

"Will do."

SWIPE WRITE
Yvonne Phillips

Gladys was running behind schedule, so I took a chair in the salon's waiting area. The woman next to me swiped madly at her phone. So fierce was one of her swipes that the phone flew from her hand and skittered across the floor.

"Damn," she muttered as she heaved herself out of the chair and picked it up.

"Sorry, I didn't intend to cause a ruckus, but last night, I joined this online dating service, and I'm trying to get the hang of swiping. I really wanted to connect with this guy, but I swiped left instead of right, and now he's gone. Damn!"

Being the only one there, she had to be talking to me. Unsure of what comment to make, I stammered, "Maybe he'll show up again."

"Nah, I don't think so. But he was a keeper for sure. Do you do online dating?"

What a personal question! But despite her bad manners, I stammered a reply. "No, I'm not even sure how online dating works."

"It's easy. All you do is fill out a questionnaire, submit a picture, and pay a small fee. Then, voila, you're active on the dating website. It's fun and helps pass the time during our lonely nights here in the mountains. Big Bear isn't exactly a dating paradise if you know what I mean."

While Gladys painted my toes, I thought about what the woman in the waiting area said. I'd been thinking about a project, and this might be it. I'd do some research, possibly write an article on my results, and submit it to the senior magazine where I'd worked before retiring.

Research finished, I called Janet. She was one of the few people I knew who still worked at *Silver Shadows.* It had helped pave the way for a slew of senior magazines that began publication in the '80s.

"Hi, Janet, it's Carol Foster."

"Carol, how the heck are you? I was just thinking about you the other day and was going to call you. What's up?"

I explained my idea of an article about seniors, anyone over fifty-five, and online dating. She thought it would be a hoot.

"Let me know when it's ready. I'll drop a couple of hints about what you're doing. The editor in charge of articles will probably love it. He likes new ideas, but he'll want your bio and other articles you've published. I never knew you were a writer and an HR expert."

"Well, there's the rub. I've published nothing. English was my major in college, but when Jim and I got married, and I became pregnant, I dropped out of school."

"Hmm, that might be a problem. He's busy and only deals with experienced writers with a track record of magazine articles. But I'll ask him and let you know." We chatted for a few more minutes and agreed to meet for lunch soon.

I returned to the computer, filled out the questionnaire, paid for a six-month subscription, and sat back and waited. It wasn't long before they emailed, saying they needed a picture of me and that my application was on hold until I supplied one.

I checked the computer and phone but found nothing suitable. Still browsing through Facebook, a 'Memory' popped up with a picture of me from maybe ten years ago. I'd had a glamour photo taken when Jim and I were going through bad times. I'd hoped it would add a little spice back into our relationship. Little did I know he was getting all the spice he wanted at work.

The picture, done with the correct make-up and lighting, clothes, and hairstyle, was flattering. You'd have never known it was me if you'd seen it and then seen me at the market with jeans, a tee shirt, no makeup, and my hair pulled up in a ponytail. Perhaps I'm the one who let the romance in our marriage die.

"STOP self-shaming!" I remembered the marriage counselor's words after all these years, and she'd been right. It takes two to ruin a marriage, one subtle and one forthright. Communication is vital, and if that's lacking, it's sometimes easy for the honeymoon express to leave the rails.

No matter, this was the only picture I had. I uploaded it to the website and went for a walk.

* * *

The small, barbequed steak and salad were delicious, as was the glass of red wine. I washed up the dishes, poured another glass of wine, opened my laptop, and logged into my account.

My picture had seventeen likes. I sorted through them. Besides looking at their pictures, I read their short bios. This was going to be more difficult than I'd imagined.

How many men should I agree to meet? After all, for me, this was only research for an article.

I tossed and turned all night, and pounding my pillow into a more comfortable lump didn't help. I was so hot I kicked off the covers, normal for a woman my age. Then, I got chilled and pulled them up. Finally, after deciding on a course of action, I fell into an exhaustive sleep.

The Unspoken Law of Three was a headline on the Internet that caught my eye. After reading the article, I decided that from the responses, I'd choose three men. Exchange texts or private messages, chat on the phone and agree to meet them.

After more swiping and reading, I decided on three:

Number One: His online name was 'Parrothead,' I wondered if he had a big beak. His status said single, never married. Worked in the insurance industry as a claims adjuster. A birder.

Number Two: Alias said, 'Colorbeyondthelines.' His choice of name made me think he liked to push boundaries. Divorced. Did he push those boundaries, too? He was a painting contractor, the custodial parent of two children, coached boys' baseball, and drove his daughter to her dance lessons.

Number Three: 'InTheStacks' works in the communications industry. Single, never married, likes to read. Hmm, probably a librarian. I yawned, then looked at his picture again. Handsome, maybe he meant haystacks.

I started with Parrothead. "Hello. Thanks for the heart."

He immediately wrote back. Geez, had he been sitting at the computer waiting for someone to reply? I knew I wasn't the only one he'd sent a heart to.

"Hello, 'Soup2Nuts.' Thanks for getting back to me. Your page didn't have too much information about you. Do you have any hobbies?"

Hmm, I hadn't thought about questions they might ask. "I do a little writing, poetry mostly."

"That's nice, and I didn't have to ask twice. I guess there's a little poetry in me, too." He sent a giggly emoji.

Oh, brother, this was going nowhere. To hurry things up, I asked him about birding. And, like all men, if you get them on a subject they're interested in, they go on and on. We messaged for about an hour. He told me more about birds than I ever wanted to know. But when he launched onto the subject of Big Bear's eagles, my interest picked up.

"Before Shadow and Jackie, Big Bear had a mating pair named Lucy and Ricky. Other eagles have come and gone, and very few are banded, so it's hard to determine where they went."

"Surprisingly, our current female eagle, Jackie, had her first nest with an eagle named Mr. B, and they had a son named Stormy. One day, another male eagle showed up. Jackie, Mr. B, and Stormy tried to chase him away but were unsuccessful. That eagle, now known as Shadow, became Jackie's new mate."

Wow, a real Big Bear soap opera going on in the treetops. Who knew?

He asked me to call him Larry and asked if we could text again. I agreed, and we set a date for the following week.

He explained our website had a phone feature that didn't let either party see the other party's number. He knew so much about it that this couldn't possibly be his first experience with swiping right.

* * *

A few days later, I responded to 'Colorbeyondthelines.' "Hello, Color. Thanks for the like. Sorry, I took so long to get back to you."

Nothing. Hmm, if he didn't contact me by morning, I'd reach out to one of the backups. Later that evening, my computer pinged.

"Hi, glad you reached out. I've been busy with work and the kids."

I glanced at his bio. Yep, it said single dad to a son and daughter and that he coached boys' baseball. He'd listed his age as fifty-three. He must have gotten a really late start. We were the same age, and my kids had already graduated college.

"Sounds like you lead a hectic life."

"You're right. Do you have kids? I don't remember from your bio if you said you had any."

"Yes, two. But mine are out of school and live off the hill."

"Really? How old are you?"

The hairs on my neck stood up, and a flash of anger spread through me. Who in the hell did this guy think he was talking to? I took a deep breath before answering.

"We're the same age. I just started my family sooner than you did."

"Yep. I'm looking at your picture. You're very attractive, even though you're a senior citizen." He chuckled. "I rarely date women my age. Seems I'm drawn to the younger ones. In fact, I never wanted kids. But the trophy wife did, so there we go."

I seethed. This was a mistake. This guy was such a jerk; I felt sorry for his children. But my curiosity got the better of me, and I asked what had happened to his wife.

He said he'd be right back. He had to go to the head. Crude! I used the time to pour another glass of wine, a large one.

"Back. Now, where were we?"

"I asked what happened to your wife."

"Oh, yeah. She was younger than me by quite a bit."

"How much younger?"

"Twenty-five years."

I almost spit out the wine I'd just sipped. Holy cow!

"Was this your first marriage?"

"No, my second. I was still married to Nancy when I met Carla."

Not caring what he thought, I blurted out, "So you cheated on your first wife and married someone a quarter of a century younger than you?"

He was silent for a bit. I thought maybe he'd finished with the contact. After all, we'd just met online; none of this was any of my business.

"Carla and I met on a job site. She took care of the people's indoor plants and fish tank. Carla was sexy as hell, wearing little short-shorts. She'd bend over from the waist and pretend to pick something up from the floor. I got the hint hard and fast. But we're divorced now. So, you want to meet up sometime, maybe go out for dinner? I like talking to you. You're a good listener. Besides, it might be nice going out with someone older for a change. I'm getting tired of dating these baseball moms. Most are only a little older than Carla, and I'm not as young as I used to be, if you know what I mean."

This was unexpected, completely out of the blue. I was still stuck on the image of Carla wearing short-shorts and wiggling her butt at him.

"Yes, I'll go out to dinner with you." I couldn't believe I'd actually uttered those words.

"Great, I knew you would. The pickins are slim up here, especially for women of your age. I'll be in touch. Oh, and my name is Pete. My business is under Peter Cummings Plumbing."

The screen went blank, and I was at a complete loss as to why I'd said yes.

* * *

My cell rang. That was unusual. Mostly, I used my landline, and all my friends knew to call me on that. Probably a spam call. "Hello."

"Hi, Carol, this is Janet. I talked to Landen, and he's interested in your article. He wants to know when you think you can have it ready for him."

My heart skipped a beat. This was wonderful. "I've completed two of the 'interviews' and only have one to go. I'd say a couple of weeks. Do you think that would be okay?"

"I don't know. It's probably better if you communicate directly with him; I'll give you his email address." She said she'd tell him I'd be in touch. We made a date for lunch at the end of the month and hung up.

Knowing that time was of the essence, I contacted 'InTheStacks,' and asked if he was still interested in chatting. It had been a week, and I wasn't sure if he'd respond, but he did.

"Good afternoon; of course, I'm still interested in communicating with you."

Wow, he sounded almost formal. "That's right, you're in the communication industry. What do you do exactly?" At first, I thought he was a Librarian, but now, after looking at his picture again I imagined he worked for the phone company, a lineman maybe. His photo showed a bearded man in aviator glasses and a cowboy hat.

"Well ... I help people communicate."

Mysterious, I liked that. I shivered when I imagined him hiking a pole and connecting broken lines thirty to forty feet up.

"Tell me, 'Soup2Nuts,' what do you do to occupy your day?"

His words were so different from the others. What did his voice sound like?

"I'm active in the local women's club, the garden club, and the mountain music committee. I also write what I hope are interesting articles and submit them to magazines."

"Something told me you'd keep yourself busy. Have they shown any interest?"

"Not yet, but I'm working on something interesting now."

"Is it about your online dating experience?"

God, how did he guess that? How should I reply? Tell the truth? Hedge or outright lie. I decided to lie. I wasn't good at lying. I never did it or rarely did it. But it ought to be easy since all of this was online.

"Are you still there?" he asked.

"Oh, yes, sorry, someone called me. I told them I'd call them back." *Lying already, look how easy it was.* "No, I'm not writing about this online experience. My article is about girls who go through the women's club's STEM program and how that program changed their lives."

"Sounds exciting." Okay, a dry sense of humor. I liked that.

"What do you do for fun?" Geez, neither Larry nor Peter asked me about fun. They only talked about themselves. I didn't want him to think I was boring or to sign off, never to be heard from again.

"Sometimes I smoke pot. It's not too much, though, just for recreation only once in a great while. It makes me laugh."

What was wrong with me? Pot was my deep, dark secret. What if he was a cop? I might get arrested. No, that was in the past; it's legal in California now.

"I'm afraid I have to cut this short. I didn't know you were going to message me, and I have a meeting in a few minutes. Hopefully, we can connect later when we both have more time. It was nice talking to you."

Damn, now he thought I was a drug addict. A pothead or a stoner. He'd been the most interesting and mysterious man I'd talked to in years.

Weeks passed (two) with no communication from 'InTheStacks.' Every time I checked my page, rejection reared its ugly head. Larry communicated frequently and invited me to go birding with him. I was giving it serious consideration.

For the benefit of my article, I checked Peter's Facebook page and looked at his pictures and his friend's pictures. Now, I was a stalker.

His former wife, Carla, was a tall blond with big hair, big eyes, and a pouty mouth. She'd moved to Florida. It was amazing how much information you could find out about someone online. All the online pictures of Peter showed him with his arm around a Carla double. He certainly had a type, and I wasn't it.

The articles were coming along slowly, though I made them as truthful and exciting as possible. I sent a rough draft to Landen's email. He briefly replied that he was deep into a series they were running, and I could take my time. But he said he'd like more on the communications character.

Okay, with orders from my editor, I contacted 'InTheStacks' again.

"Hi, it's been a few weeks since I last checked my account," *Liar, liar.* "And I'm wondering if you still want to communicate or if I should just swipe on by."

Total amazement. He answered.

"Glad you reached out. I've been swamped at work."

I watched the weather religiously and knew parts of the country were suffering from severe summer storms. If he were a lineman for the phone company, he'd have been plenty busy. Heck, I didn't even know where he lived.

"I know how that is." *In reality, I had no idea. My HR job had been mundane.*

"What do you think about getting together for coffee or a drink?"

My stomach did flip-flops. *Play it cool; don't let him know how anxious you are to meet up.* "I've never done this online dating before, but I suppose that would be ok. I'm still working on that article on the STEM girls. So, I think a drink after work would probably be best."

"That's fine. How about The Rusty Nail, Friday at 6:30?"

"You picked the place with the best views of the lake. Do you live on the mountain?"

"No, not exactly, but I know my way around up there. I ski a lot in the winter."

"How am I going to know who you are?" *Be still my heart; I'd memorized his picture with the beard and cowboy hat.*

"You'll know, I'll surprise you. Besides, I know what you look like. I saw your picture, remember?"

Oh yeah, my glamour photo from ten years ago. "I've changed my hairstyle."

"That's fine, and I have a good eye. See you Friday evening."

* * *

A line began to form at the hostess' podium. She looked up, "Do you have a reservation?"

Did we? I'd give it a go, "Party of two for…" hell, I didn't even know his name. I gave it my best shot. "Stacks, a party of two for Stacks."

She glanced at her reservation list, looked at me, and smiled. "Yes, here you are. I'll seat you in the bar while you wait for Mr. Stacks."

The waitress asked what I'd like. Hesitating, I ordered a glass of house cabernet. Scanning the crowd while I sipped my wine, I saw several men come in alone. Each time, wondering if that was him. Had he used an old picture as I had, or maybe someone else?

The door opened, and a red balloon tied with a ribbon floated in before its holder.

The man said something to the hostess. She looked my way and nodded. I gave a little wave. A tall man with a beard but no cowboy hat or aviator glasses followed her to the table.

He gave the balloon to the hostess and slid into the chair across from me. Graceful for a big man, nice.

"It's nice to finally meet you. You're as beautiful as your picture." I'd imagined his voice many times, and it didn't disappoint.

My cheeks warmed. *How long had it been since I'd blushed? Years.* "It's nice to meet you too." *You look as handsome as your picture, I almost blurted out.*

I wanted to find out more about him. He was handsome, but who was he, what was he like inside, how did he treat people, and why wasn't he already taken? The evening turned into night, and we ordered dinner. We were never without words, and the conversation flowed smoothly.

At nine, a man at the piano and another on base started to play. People began to fill the small dance floor. He reached for my hand. "Would you like to dance?"

I nodded. A long time had passed since I'd danced with anyone. But when I slid into his arms, it seemed like the most natural thing in the world.

He walked me to my car. *Was he going to kiss me? I wouldn't mind if he did. In fact, I wanted him to.*

We stood facing each other. "I had a good time tonight," he said. "I'm glad we met. If you'd like, maybe we could do this again. And from now on, call me Dawson."

"I'd like that." He pulled me close, and I turned my face up, awaiting his kiss, but he only held me close for a moment and then let me go. Opening the car door, he told me to drive carefully, said he'd be in touch, turned, and walked away.

What the hell? Did I have lettuce in my teeth or something? All the way home, his words echoed in my memory. "Maybe we could do this again?" I thought the night had gone wonderfully, but obviously, he hadn't.

Too wound up to sleep, I pounded out the rest of my Online Dating Experiences article. This last part was all about him. After doing a quick edit, I sent it off to Landen.

I didn't hear from Dawson again. That left a sad place in my heart. Communication with Larry slowed to a crawl, and Peter was a no-show.

Would I try online dating again? I could; after all, my account was still active. And one of these lonely mountain nights, I just might.

A few weeks later, I received an email from Landen that he wanted me to come to his office to discuss the article. His office was in Victorville, about forty minutes away.

I'd been expecting to drive to LA. It was news to me they had an office in Victorville, but then again, I'd been retired for five years.

The sign on the sizeable six-story building said JDL International Publishing. It was one of the tallest buildings in the area. To my knowledge, Silver Singles was only an American-published magazine.

Things certainly had changed in five years. I parked in the lot and took the elevator to the sixth floor.

The elevator doors opened into a large reception area. It was nice, very modern. I gave the receptionist my name, and she directed me down the hall to Landen's office. I tapped lightly on the door.

"Come in."

Inside the huge office was a wall-to-wall, floor-to-ceiling bookcase filled with books. Landon sat behind a large desk with his back to the office door. He was typing on a large screen computer.

"Sorry about this; it's a last-minute detail." He coughed.

Holy cow, I hoped I didn't catch anything.

"About this cough, I've been ill, not Covid, just a bad cold, but it's just a scratchy throat now. Come on in and have a seat. I'll be right with you."

I sat, folded my hands in my lap, and continued to survey my surroundings. The office, beautifully decorated, must have cost a fortune. I tried to remember how much they paid for an article.

I didn't notice that he'd swung around and sat watching me. My breath caught in my throat.

"Dawson! What are you doing here?!" My mind spun. Of course, now that I put it together. Dawson is 'Stacks' real name. Landen is his editing name—the initials on the building JDL Publishing.

I stood. "Please don't go. I love your article, and we want to publish it."

"Did you know who I was when we met at The Rusty Nail?"

I didn't care that they wanted to publish my article. It would be my first published piece and could lead to other magazines and stories. But I was beyond angry.

"Yes, of course, I knew who you were. I only opened that online account because I liked the premise of your article. Luckily, I used the right app. I was delighted when you swiped on my picture. I really wanted to meet you, but I bided my time, not wanting to scare you off. Please forgive me for the subterfuge."

I sat, my feelings mixed. Angry at being lied to and that Dawson hadn't told me who he was at dinner that night. But I was flattered that he wanted to meet me and liked my article. Silence filled the room. I'm not usually at a loss for words, but I didn't know what to say.

"Can you forgive me?" I loved his voice. It flowed over me like a satin shawl.

What did I have to gain by rebuffing his offer to publish my article? Nothing. "I suppose."

"Good. I'll call my secretary and have her collect the contract from legal. Feel free to have your attorney review the contract before signing it. I'd like to buy you lunch to celebrate our new business venture. Are you free?"

What could I say? That I had a lunch date with a Costco hot dog and soda? "Yes, I'm free, and I'd like to join you for lunch. Very much."

PHANTOM RICHES

Karene Horst

Grant poked at the fire with the iron stoker, sending a shower of sparks spiraling up toward the chimney.

From a few steps away, a voice purred to him. "Honey, stop messing with that fire." Cherry patted the space on the threadbare sofa next to her. She believed this last-minute weekend getaway meant he had bought the ring and mustered the nerve to propose.

Grant fixed his gaze on the flames flaring from the logs in the stone fireplace. "Hey," he glanced over his shoulder at her as he continued to prod the burning wood with the sharp end of the long stoker. "Did you see that brochure I left on the coffee table? I found it in the rack at the rental office."

Cherry reached for the black and white pamphlet. "Ghost Hunting in Big Bear," she read out loud.

"Hmmmph," she snorted with exasperation. She glared at the blurry photos and bullet points highlighting guided tours of a "haunted cabin" and jeep rides through a nearby "ghost town" of old mining structures and other "frightening historic sites." Not Cherry's idea of a romantic weekend.

She tossed the brochure back onto the scuffed tabletop with a dismissive shrug of her shoulders. "You know I'm not into ghosts or any of that silly nonsense. How about a hot tub? Didn't you say this place had one?"

Cherry had no interest in braving the elements outside for a dip in a hot tub, as the wind had grown stronger soon after they entered the tiny log cabin.

The crisp October afternoon had descended into a blustery, dark night. A hot tub could be romantic, but not in this weather, Cherry noted to herself. She only mentioned it to Grant so she could distract him from playing with the fire or fantasizing about foolish things. She wanted him sitting beside her, cuddling her and treating her like precious treasure as she deserved. Or even better, bending the knee at her feet and begging her to say "Yes."

"Sure, we can do a tub," Grant said in a bland voice. Then his tone rose with enthusiasm. "But just think, these mountains have a crazy history. Lots of insane things happened here! This was the old Wild, Wild West–miners and claim jumpers and outlaws and saloons with dance hall girls. Old cemeteries, a tree they used to hang murderers and criminals. Maybe even some innocent of whatever somebody accused them of. I bet a lot of unhappy spirits wander around these hills."

"Oh please, spare me your weirdness."

Cherry loved so many things about Grant, but his childish fascination with the paranormal annoyed her. During their last weekend trip to San Diego, he talked her into a visit to the "haunted" Whaley House. So hokey and boring. He did not propose to her then, and after she woke up in a snit Sunday morning, they motored back to Riverside in silence. She pinned her hopes on this weekend. If he refused to step up to the plate, she would have to give him the ultimatum.

"So you don't believe in ghosts," Grant said in all seriousness as if he did not already fully grasp her opinion on the subject.

"Oh Grant, you like chasing ghosts, I like online shopping. I don't subject you to staring at my computer screen every time I order a new pair of shoes."

"But you do make me 'oooh' and 'ahhh' over every new dress you try on."

Grant sighed. The weekend had only begun and the inevitable bickering along with it. "How about a night out then? We could drive to the Village. There's this restaurant …"

Cherry threw him a menacing look. "I'm not going to that restaurant they say is haunted by some guy who killed himself …"

"OK, OK. Then we'll have a quiet night in. We can order pizza. They've got DoorDash up here. Domino's. It's sort of cold and windy out anyway."

As if to emphasize his point, a branch thwacked the side of the cabin. Then a pine cone plummeting from high above hit the roof like a bomb before tumbling noisily down the shingles.

"What was that?" Cherry squealed.

"Hmm, could be poor ol' one-armed miner Legless Jack, dragging himself around until he can claw his way in …"

Cherry rolled her eyes. "You need to work on handing me a slice of cheese and pepperoni pizza and a glass of wine. I feel I've earned at least that after the awful long and winding drive up here."

Suddenly, all the lights shut off.

"Ooooooh," Grant moaned with exaggeration in an eerie voice.

"Stop that. Stop that, Grant. Stop teasing me. What just happened?"

"The wind probably knocked a power line out of commission. I hear it happens in these mountains a lot, especially when the weather kicks up. Besides, we've got the fire to keep the demons and goblins at bay."

Grant made his way toward the kitchen drawers and searched with his hands for a flashlight. He felt nothing resembling a flashlight, only an assortment of kitchen utensils, paper clips, plastic bags, and the book of matches he used earlier to start the fire.

He pulled his cell phone from his vest pocket but discovered he had no signal. He switched to Wi-Fi calling but realized that with the power outage they did not have any internet connection either. He focused on the bright screen, watching his phone's tiny icon spin in its endless cycle. Completely useless.

Cherry grabbed for her cell phone encased in a rhinestone-studded cover. She stabbed her finger at the screen before tossing it back onto the coffee table.

"But … how will we … what about ordering pizza, what about dinner?" Cherry pleaded.

The firelight flickering over her face mottled her features. For an instant, Grant sensed that Cherry's face had begun melting away. He fluttered his eyes and shook his head as if to throw off this disturbing image.

Furious gusts buffeted the windows and Cherry screeched.

"Grant, I'm scared. Why don't we have any electricity, any cell phone service? What if a tree falls on top of us? What if something happens? We're out here all alone. No neighbors. Why did you pick this remote cabin, you know I'm afraid of the dark!"

No, she never told him that before. Good to know, Grant thought to himself.

"Why do you have to constantly subject me to your stupid obsession with ghosts and abandoned places out in the middle of nowhere?"

Grant grimaced.

Then the windowpanes and the glasses in the kitchen cabinets rattled for a few seconds.

Cherry's voice pitched even higher, "Grant! This is horrible. What was that?"

"An earthquake, just a tiny earthquake. We live in California, remember?" He tried to muffle the irritation in his voice.

The wind groaned as it circled the cabin. A falling branch bashed onto the roof. The explosion from the impact startled Cherry and she whimpered.

Pillars of air blasted down the chimney, almost extinguishing the tiny fire Grant had managed to coax to life. *Egads, if the fire goes out all hell will break loose.* Then he persuaded himself to comfort his unhinged girlfriend. *You've still got all weekend. Don't blow it right out the gate.*

He joined her on the couch, feigning sympathy by wrapping his arms around her, patting her shoulders, and calming her with trite words and banal phrases as if she were a child awakened by a nightmare.

She rested her head against his shoulder, clinging to him with her small, expertly manicured hands. After a few soothing minutes, she smiled. "You're so sweet to me," she hummed. He grinned as he eased away from his benevolent, reassuring hug and started rubbing her back, caressing her arms, kissing the top of her salon-styled head of hair before tilting his head downward to nuzzle her neck.

Then something caught his eye outside beyond the front window. Something shimmered. *Is that a light?* It appeared fuzzy as if shrouded by a mist or light fog. It swung side to side slightly. Then it rose a few feet before dropping back to its previous position. Grant caught his breath. He watched the light for a few more seconds as it meandered into nothingness. He yanked himself away from Cherry.

"What is it, sweetie?"

Grant muttered something incomprehensible.

Confused, he speculated on the source of this odd sight. *Who could be outside this isolated cabin, rambling through the woods at night in a horrendous storm? Could someone be lost, maybe a missing hiker? Was someone in trouble?*

A sense of unease flooded him and made him blink. He clenched his jaw as he considered a reasonable explanation for what he had just seen. He wondered if he should check it out.

The wind wailed. To Grant, it almost sounded human, as if someone beyond the cabin shouted, calling for help maybe? His spine tingled.

He could open the door and step outside onto the porch. "Who's out there? Who's there?" he could roar in a challenging tone. Or he could offer assistance in a firm, authoritative voice. He could not come across as upset or weak. He did not have a clue as to where the owners stashed a flashlight. Even if he could find a candle to light, one gust would have smothered the flame instantly.

The storm rumbled haphazardly about the one-bedroom cabin. Another branch or some heavy object slammed against the wooden structure. Grant shivered. The thought of roaming outside in this harsh, unforgiving landscape to explore the mysterious unknown suddenly lost its appeal. He scrunched his face, puzzled as he considered his next move. He rose from the couch, shuffled toward the window, and peered out. He could recognize shadows, blurry stands of weeds, low shrubs, and tree limbs wrestling with the wind. A tremor ran through his body, then a chill. Goosebumps sprouted on his arms.

"I thought I saw something," Grant mumbled.

He edged away from the window and looked at the door. Did they lock it?

"What are you doing? What's out there? Come back here now! Don't leave me on the couch here by myself. I'm scared! You're scaring me!"

The terror in Cherry's voice grabbed Grant by the throat and he suddenly felt like screaming. Then Grant's eyes twitched. As if snapping out of hypnosis, he abruptly clapped his hands together.

"Nothing. I think it's the altitude. Never mind me. Let's slice up the hunk of cheese you brought. That and some crackers and some wine. We don't need to order pizza."

"No, come here. Come here now. I need you," she whined.

"OK, you asked for it, here I come." He hopped over the sofa's padded arm and sprawled on the end opposite Cherry. She erupted in nervous laughter, unnaturally loud and grating, as he scooted sideways and settled in next to her.

He felt Cherry squirm against him as if she could meld her body closer to his. Grant buried his anxiety over the strange light outside, the unnatural sound echoing through the forest. A half-smile crept across his lips. Grant's idea of a "romantic weekend" did not include a marriage proposal.

Suddenly the lights flared. They both flinched, recoiling from each other's embrace. They blinked rapidly as their eyes adjusted to the brightness. Grant peeked at the front window. Only the interior lights reflected off the opaque glass.

"Oh thank god the electricity is back on," Cherry cried out. "Let me check my phone … nope, still no service. Oh, how awful. I hope that doesn't happen again. We'll have to complain to the management. What if the lights hadn't turned back on?"

Grant laughed maniacally. "Maybe we would have had to fight off the ghoulish specter of some old geezer, murdered by a claim jumper …"

"Oh stop it, Grant just quit! I'm already creeped out as it is!"

* * *

"Etta! Etta girl, where the heck are ya?" Henry hollered.

But the wind snatched his words and hurled them away. He raised his oil lantern by the metal handle and peered through the darkness. The lantern swayed with the wind but barely illuminated the grove of western junipers he almost wandered into. The weak glow from the lantern did not show Henry where his pack mule Etta had escaped to. He lowered his arm as he hunched forward to shoulder against the violent gale determined to fling him into a ravine like a leafless limb broken off a dead oak tree.

The prospector kicked at a clump of weeds. He staggered, not just because of the powerful winds pummeling him or the rough ground he traversed, but from the drink. He celebrated his discovery, a thin shimmering line in the rock peeking out between the layers of quartz and stone and ore he worked for the past month. A gold seine. He dug out a small clump, large enough to keep him in vittles and whiskey for a month but not big enough to alert the thieves and claim jumpers who would slit his throat in order to steal his find.

He planned on filing his claim the following day. But tonight he would toast his future. Then he heard a loud bang and a smashing racket out back, and Etta unleashed a braying and a heehawing. By the time he jammed his feet into his leather boots, loaded his shotgun, and grabbed his oil lamp, she was gone. Something knocked over the tiny corral he had patched together out of narrow tree trunks and thick limbs up against his one-room wooden shanty.

Henry cursed as a fierce blast threw him off balance and shoved him into a sharp-needled pinyon tree. *Why the heck did Etta run off? Did something lurking in the forest spook her? A grizzly or a pack of coyotes maybe?* All she needed to do was sound the alarm and Henry would have shot at anything or anyone meaning to do her harm. He depended on her to haul his prospecting tools–pickax, shovel, chisel, hammer, gold pan–along with his loaded shotgun across the rocky terrain. He counted on her to carry his provisions from the store when he trekked into the mining camp to resupply: the heavy sacks of flour and dried beans; smaller sacks of coffee, sugar, and salt; a large block of lard for making biscuits and fueling his oil lantern; maybe some bacon or salt pork if he had not picked off a squirrel or a rabbit; a jug of whiskey now and again. Once he sweet-talked Etta into hauling a deer he bagged, but she did not like it. In return, she could count on him to feed her a handful of grain now and then, stake her close to some grass to graze, water her, protect her with his shotgun or at least his booming voice. *She did not need to go run off like that. She knew better. Why had she run off?*

He called and called for her to return home before striking out after her. She knew the way home. She knew those trails better than Henry. But it was getting late and he was drunk and without thinking or even grabbing his wool coat and canvas hat, Henry took off to find her.

"Get on back here, Etta, or you'll get et by a mountain lion if you don't git home," he bellowed.

The wind surged, blowing harder and colder. *Storm*, he shuddered to himself as he damned the vicious squalls that attacked the mountains before disappearing with anything he forgot to cinch up or nail down. He figured he would surely lose something with this brutal weather but he could not afford to lose Etta, his only companion and helpmate. He had told her so many times, more times than he could recall, how they would hit pay dirt and how he would buy that ranch and how he would build her a nice corral and a barn full of dry straw, one with hewn planks of wood, sunk in the ground, sturdy and safe. How she would have her own pasture, fresh grain every day. Apples even. Why, he would plant an apple tree, just for her. Henry knew she understood him, just knew it, as Etta appeared to listen to him, twitching her long ears toward him, her brown eyes watching as he loaded or unloaded her bulging pack saddle.

"Etta girl, come on, come on now!" Henry spat in disgust, but the spittle only traveled as far as his whiskered chin. *Wicked cold out*, he scowled. He squinted into the gloom that his oil lamp barely cracked apart. He stumbled across the frozen ground, the wind entwining and whipping his long hair every which way until matted tufts slapped him in the face. Too drunk to feel the icy cold ripping through his linen shirt, he pressed onward.

"EEEETTTTAAAHHH!"

Weeks later a fellow prospector stumbled upon Henry's body. He had squatted on the ground for a short rest during his search for Etta, huddling against a massive boulder that provided him little protection from the blizzard.

Postscript:
The gold miners and prospectors of Holcomb Valley and the hillsides and streams surrounding Big Bear never unearthed the "mother lode" of gold. Some search for it to this day with more than 1,000 active mining claims in the area. The old prospector Henry never found his pack mule Etta, and he continues his search for her as well.

119

WHERE THERE'S SMOKE
Lori Brookes

"Is that smoke?" asked the rookie Fire Lookout Volunteer with a lump in her throat and a deer-caught-in-headlights look plastered all over her face.

That rookie was me. The long-awaited day for my in-tower training was here and I was beyond excited to earn my status as a Fire Lookout Volunteer under the US Forest Service, overseeing the safety of my town—Idyllwild, and the San Bernardino National Forest. Home. I live in a forest.

A slow day in the tower is a very good day. My trainer, Charles, a very thorough and meticulous kind of guy, patiently took us through every procedure calmly and methodically. No page of the manual was left unturned. We proudly raised the red, white, and blue, we took the weather readings, temperature, humidity, wind, and direction. Time to radio into dispatch, "San Bernardino, Tahquitz Peak, in-service with weather." The call includes our weather calculations and observations. Dispatch confirms, "Tahquitz Peak in-service at 800 hours. Good morning." We are now officially in-service!

I had many firsts that day, raised the American flag (military fold at days' end), used an official fire dispatch radio, learned to operate the vintage piece of fire detection equipment, the Osborne Firefinder, and…

We had just settled on the catwalk to take a quick break and have a bite to eat. Our lookout routine required us to scan the forest, quadrant by quadrant, every 15 minutes. Just five minutes prior, I spotted the forested grid of my old neighborhood. I could easily make out the gray asphalt line of Middle Ridge Drive cutting through the green of the trees. I could also see the side street where I had lived on the corner lot. It felt like I was reading a map in real-time from a bird's-eye view. I was thrilled to have identified at least one area in the tower's 360-degree view from 8,845 feet above sea level. Although I could identify much more, seeing my old neighborhood from this height felt incredibly exciting.

With another bite of my sandwich, I looked over again in the direction of my old neighborhood and I couldn't believe my rookie eyes. It looked like smoke billowing up over the treetops and only a few blocks from my old place. The first half of the training day we had been running smoke drills, using our tools for locating the smoke. Using high-powered binoculars, map coordinates and distances from the Osborne Firefinder, and geographical landmarks. Like my former neighborhood.

Charles, seated between me and the other trainee, continued his schooling between small bites when out of my bewildered mouth rang like a bell, "Is that smoke?" I pointed in the direction that we had only minutes before talked about. It happened that fast. Sometimes what looks like smoke isn't smoke, they are referred to as waterdogs, water vapors that if given a few minutes will dissipate. Smoke, however, doesn't behave that way. Calmly, Charles stood and brought the binoculars to eye level. I was on the edge of terror and hope, the hope that I was rookie-wrong.

All six eyes were on the smoke. This was no waterdog. Our in-tower training just went live! Charles led the real-time operation of sighting the smoke within the crosshairs of the Osborne Firefinder, while he gave us hands-on education. Together we took the azimuth reading, the distance from the tower (we are the center from which all is measured), and lastly the geographical location. My former neighborhood. The smoke was building and with our naked eyes, we could see flames. It was more than clear that this was a house fire.

With all our data gathered Charles asked if I wanted to call the smoke report into dispatch since I was the one who spotted it first. A little rattled by it all, I took that radio, pulled up my big-girl pants, and made my first smoke report to San Bernardino dispatch. Our job was done. We were the first to report that fire and it was beyond accurate, thanks to our meticulous and well-seasoned leader. Now we listen, watch, and wait. And ultimately get back to scanning the forest.

I excused myself after making that call. Adrenaline overflowed and the emotion of that event sent me to the back of the tower where I burst into tears. Three years prior I had moved to the mountains, to THAT neighborhood, I'd been unpacked for three weeks when an arsonist lit us up! The cabin I had rented, which I discovered after the return from evacuation, was 450 feet away from being burnt down along with all of my worldly possessions. I had survived the Cranston Fire but was still traumatized. I had a justified watershed moment, and Charles understood.

* * *

A longer story than can be told here moved me to the Big Bear Valley, and I transferred my Fire Lookout Volunteer post to our beloved Butler Peak Fire Lookout Tower located at 8,547 feet above sea level, on the north side of the valley. A rough-ride dirt road will get you there in about five miles.

In both cases, as fire lookout towers go, I work in two of the most unique towers in our seven-tower system. Correction, six, in September 2022, we lost one of our old gals, Red Mountain, the youngest of the tower sisters during the Fairview Fire in Hemet. A fire that ran simultaneously with the Radford Fire that was in our neck of the woods.

Tahquitz Peak is the only tower in our system that is located within a wilderness area of the national forest, and due to that location, can only be reached by hoofing it. It's a 4.2-mile trek up to serve, with an elevation gain of 2,300 feet. Different and more stringent rules exist in a wilderness area and that applies to the fire tower as well. There is no running water, no electricity, no facilities of any kind. You might be lucky to get some cell service! And even when it comes to working on the tower, all tools must be primitive hand tools. No battery-operated types are allowed. So when you work this tower, you bring all of your needs with you, on foot, in a backpack.

Butler Peak has her unique quality, different from Tahquitz Peak, as you can drive up to the foot of Butler, with a very short but steep walk up to her metal set of stairs. Butler Peak is the only tower that is not built on a stilt system giving it the presence of a tower, she is built directly on top of an outcropping of massive boulders. If you haven't been up to visit this tower, it is quite an impressive engineering accomplishment, considering it was built back in the mid-1930s.

* * *

There exists a romantic quality or maybe more appropriately, a romanticized idea, about fire lookout towers. Admittedly when I first hiked up to Tahquitz Peak and took a look inside, I dreamt of working there and doing what is called an overnighter. After the shift ends, you radio out-of-service and stay the night. A glamp out! The allure of promised solitude, 360 degree views, treasured time to read a book or write one, and oh let's not forget that tiny bed in the corner to rest your head and weary bones after a long day of watching over precious territory.

I felt in good company when learning that the likes of the Beat Generation poet and writer, Jack Kerouac, had romanticized his way into a 63-day-long stint on Desolation Peak in Washington State, as a fire lookout volunteer. He had some notion that something was going to happen to him like land an epiphany or bust out a new epic novel. Something life-changing! But as I read about this time in his life, it rendered his writings in the tower into dreary journal entries, much to do with boredom, loneliness, and his life's demons.

Nevertheless, the allure finally got me. After waiting a few months to become a more seasoned fire lookout, I took a string of solo shifts which included two back-to-back overnight stays. I brought it all, including two books, a journal, and my favorite pen. I planned to, after a long day of fire-watch duty, boil my backpacking dinner and once my appetite was curbed, I'd nestle into my little cozy corner of the fire tower cab, inspired by my surroundings I'd write away or read like no one was watching. After all, I had the place to myself.

This time of year, coming into fall, sunsets were happening around 6 p.m. and that put me in a 'squirrel' moment. Who can resist a sunset, especially when you are poised high above the clouds? Once I photographed the heck out of that, the reality of a long night ahead settled in. OK, now what? I had my books and writing material at the ready, but the sound of silence, away from everything and everyone was exquisitely loud. No distractions to speak of, except for the monkeys swinging from branch-to-branch inside my brain.

With my headlamp on (remember there is no electricity up there), I decide to bust out a deck of cards I found inside the desk drawer and play… solitaire. That lasted for a few rounds. This was a great reminder of camping out when you can't have a campfire to stare into. It's dark, I'm bored, and the night at elevation is getting cold. Bundled up warm I sink into the little, cozy-looking twin-sized bed and pull the covers over. The worst bed ever! I can feel the coil spring from the circa who-knows-what-year mattress and the squeaks from my toss-and-turn sleeping style. This proved to be a long and dark night for my soul! And I had one more to go.

The days are busily filled with fire watching but also with a few dozen hikers who journey up to visit these historical landmarks. I adore the visits and drink them up knowing what's coming after sundown when everyone has left the mountaintop and returned to their lives, complete with modern conveniences.

While I never managed to do any deep-dive journaling during my two nights, like Jack, I was definitely over the romanticized relationship between me and the tower! Back to the serious side of the tower business.

* * *

The typical fire lookout's day begins at 8:00 a.m. with our shifts ending at 5:00 p.m. The main purpose of our duty as a fire lookout is, *if* we spot smoke, and we always hope we don't, to report the location to the best of our abilities using the tools of sight, knowledge, and the off-any-grid piece of equipment, the tried-and-true Osborne Firefinder.

At Butler Peak our watch area spans to the east end of the valley, beyond Big Bear Lake to Baldwin Lake, and west past Lake Arrowhead. To the south, the north-facing walls of the San Gorgonio Wilderness Area, and looking north, the series of peaks, boulders, and summits that form the Big Bear Valley. It's quite a chunk of real estate, only realized from way up in the tower, with her endless 360 degree views. Part of our training, and it is ongoing, is to become intimately familiar with and knowledgeable of all of the terrain, the landscape, peaks, campsites, forest service roads, neighborhoods, buildings … the list goes on. These are referred to as landmarks when a smoke report is called in.

Once in-service, we start our ritual. The ritual of forest scanning. Weather permitting, every 15 minutes we take to the catwalk that borders the 14 x 14-foot vintage wooden structure known as the cab, and section-by-section we scan with our eyes, from the tops of peaks to valley floors, and every tree in between. The goal is that we see nothing, this defines a good day. Nothing but blue skies! Once the circuit is complete we get a 15-minute reprieve. Breathe in a sigh of relief, visit the facilities, eat a snack or lunch, enjoy the peace; notice nowhere did I insert—read a book! If I'm lucky I'll have intermittent visitors to the tower that will weave into the ritual. A lovely break from the monotony of a trusted routine.

Butler Peak, as with many of our lookout towers, is a relevant piece of history, a historical landmark, and as such is considered by the U.S. Forest Service a visitor center, in addition to a working fire suppression unit. This provides a wonderful educational opportunity for all who visit, along with those views! It's a balancing act to scan and educate. I probably scan more frequently than the average Smokey Bear, but it's hard not to especially after 5:00 p.m. when I'm off duty and lingering into an overnight stay … the sun is still out and so are the things and the humans that can light up a forest. My personal experience with the Cranston Fire in Idyllwild punctuates that.

I became a Fire Lookout Volunteer to be of service, especially to our vulnerable community of family, friends, and wildlife who live in the forest.

Because, where there's smoke… there's fire.

DAY OF CHANGE
Yvonne Phillips

Hubert lived a solitary life in a small apartment with no children and no wife. He liked things quiet, didn't make waves, and got along with everyone. "Do your job and keep your head down." His father's words echoed through the years. Hubert eats when he's hungry, watches TV when he wants, and goes to bed when sleepy. There's no one to please but himself.

Then, one day, everything changed.

It began the morning when he had no coffee filters. Darn. Hubert remembered writing them on his shopping list, but the day he'd done his marketing, he'd left the list at home. What to do? He needed his morning coffee! Jerking a paper towel from the roll, only a tiny piece broke off, not enough for a filter. He yanked the roll harder; it came out of its holder and spilled into the damp sink. It was his only roll. Taking a deep breath, he tore off enough to cut a correct-sized circle, measured the coffee, turned on the pot, and went to shower. However, he'd forgotten to add water. The empty glass pot overheated, shattering into a gazillion pieces that spewed onto the counter and kitchen floor.

He cleaned up the mess. That caused him to run late. He hurried to catch the bus, but he was behind schedule. As he turned the corner, the bus spit exhaust from its rear pipe and rumbled down the street without him.

Today, of all days, the security guard at the company's entrance carefully checked everyone's ID. Strange, he usually only gave it a cursory glance. A long line of employees formed. Most joking and talking, Hubert fumed this would ruin his attendance record. He'd never been late, not in twenty-eight years. The morning's disruptions to his routine caused dots of perspiration to pepper his forehead.

Once at his desk, he felt better. He pulled a clean white handkerchief from his pocket and blotted away the morning irritations. A gasp came from a cubicle near the end of his row of cubicles at the far end of the accounting floor. Maybe they'd just reached their desk and were taking a deep breath. Hubert turned on his computer, and his world changed.

Fox Unlimited Accounting is proud to announce we are now part of Hudson Securities Inc. All employees will meet with HR before the week's end.

His stomach flip-flopped. Collective gasps sprang from nearby cubicles. People rose from their chairs, formed small groups, and talked in hushed voices. Hubert typed madly on his computer.

By the end of the week, three-quarters of the company had visited HR. More than a few came back teary-eyed and cleaned out their desks. Though not a betting man, Hubert started making bets with himself about who would clean out their desks and who would not. He was right ninety-nine percent of the time. The fifty-year-olds and older were leaving in droves. Though he wasn't yet fifty, he was close and figured he, too, would be leaving.

He'd prepared himself for his meeting with Human Resources and had already cleaned out his meager personal items. They said the usual platitudes that wouldn't get them an age discrimination lawsuit, and, although he'd been there almost thirty years, he received nothing, not even a week's pay in lieu of the vacation he was due and certainly not a golden parachute like the senior partner of the company received.

Hubert arrived home before noon. It was the first time that had happened in almost thirty years. An envelope was taped to his door. Venting the day's frustrations, he tore open the envelope. The building's owners were returning to the city and wanted his apartment. Enclosed was a thirty-day notice.

* * *

The amber liquid looked inviting. Though not a drinker, Hubert raised the glass to his lips, savoring the slow burn of the good whiskey. Delicious. Pouring another, he left the bottle on the table.

He pondered his life while the whiskey seared a trail down his throat. Despite its hustle and bustle and hordes of people crowding the subways and sidewalks, New York City was a lonely place— millions of souls locked in their little cubicle lives, at work and in life.

Did he want to spend the rest of his time on this earth locked away as he had been for years? Or, deep down, did he yearn for something more? Hubert had already decided to never again work for a huge, uncaring monolith of a company. But he needed to decide where he'd live. If he were to change his life, he'd do it thoroughly.

No one who knew him would have expected what happened next.

Taking a United States Atlas from the shelf, he laid it on the table. He was about to make a life-changing decision and needed a moment. Hubert put his hands on top of it and closed his eyes.

He thought of his plan for some time, nodded to himself, and, with eyes still closed, opened the book.

Then he blindly pointed to a spot where he'd spend the rest of his life. Opening his eyes, he saw he'd landed in California. He looked closer and saw the bold name: Los Angeles. Not bad, no more slush and snow. But his finger was north and a little east of L.A. He picked up a magnifying glass. A spot of blue shone back at him, and in tiny letters, it said, 'Big Bear Lake.'

Moving from one coast to another wouldn't be easy. And since Hubert had lived in one place for many years, his accumulated treasures proved to be many. He needed to be practical about taking things he'd never use, such as the full dinnerware service for eight that his mother left him. She'd been so proud of it, collecting a free piece with every twenty dollars she'd spent at the market. In the end, Hubert couldn't bring himself to give the dishes away. So, he packed them.

His mother's car was old but only had twenty thousand miles on the odometer. He'd kept it in a storage garage his mother had purchased years ago.

He used to take his mother for a drive every Sunday. And since she'd passed, he drove it several times a year, not only for the car's good but to keep up his driving skills.

Before his cross-country adventure, he had it serviced and bought new tires. Hubert wanted to take his time venturing across the county and didn't want any car problems. He'd taken several guided tours through Europe but never explored the United States. The Grand Canyon was at the top of his list of things to see.

Hubert invested many hours online, trading emails about Big Bear Lake properties with real estate agents. He looked forward to seeing the house he'd bought sight unseen.

* * *

The crisp mountain air and golden leaves of the oaks told all that fall had arrived. The sky was the bluest he'd ever enjoyed, with small puffy clouds floating far above the treetops. Hubert sniffed the air, unable to identify the smell. In time, he'd recognize it as wood smoke. It drifted through the valley with the lighting of the fireplaces.

Though he'd always been thrifty and invested in the stock market, Hubert had never owned real estate. He silently thanked his mother, who had invested in that Manhattan garage despite his father's grumbling. His broker had gotten a quarter of a million dollars for it, which helped him afford this mountain cabin.

"A leopard can't change its spots," the idiom popped into Hubert's mind. He decided he'd prove the old saying wrong. After all, he'd moved across the country, was a freelance CPA, and owned real estate—all things he'd never done before.

He bought hiking boots, paying a fortune for comfortable ones. Hubert purchased an electric mountain bike. Although he hadn't ridden a bike in ages, he'd always heard you never forget how to ride. And at a yard sale, he purchased a paddle board. He vowed to learn how to use it next summer.

The Roar of the Greasepaint—The Smell of the Crowd, one of his favorite Broadway shows, had featured a song that kept running through his mind. It was a new day, and Hubert felt good, a new dawn

for the rest of his life. He turned on his Bluetooth®
and sang along out loud.

"Hey, mister, what are you doing up there? You
practicin' being in a play or somethen?" A boy,
holding the hand of a younger one, stared up at him
from the road.

Embarrassed to have been caught singing aloud,
even by two little boys, Hubert stuttered out an
answer. "No, I'm just singing a song I like."

"We were in a play up here at the PAC," said the
talkative one while they climbed the stairs to the
deck.

Hubert had no experience dealing with children,
except maybe delivery boys when he ordered food if
he was sick. But these guys were far from teenagers.
He guessed the bigger one to be around ten. But he
could have been a large seven-year-old or a small
twelve-year-old. Hubert had no idea.

Reaching the deck, the boys stood and stared at him.
"Mr. Asher used to live here. He died. I saw them take
his body away. They put it in a big white bag with a

zipper. The police were here and put up yellow crime scene tape and everything."

Hubert vaguely remembered the real estate agent saying something about someone dying in the house, but she hadn't mentioned the police. "Had Mr. Asher been sick?" He couldn't help himself, though it seemed to be a weird conversation to be having with a child.

"No, talk is someone pushed him down the stairs. He hit his head. There was a big pool of blood. Is it still there? Can I see it?" The bigger boy headed for the front door.

"Ah, no, it's not there anymore, if it ever was, and you can't go in my house. Who are you anyway? Where did you come from? And didn't your parents ever tell you not to talk to strangers?" He knew the last part sounded rude but needed to be the adult here.

"My name's Danny. This is my little brother Toby. We live up the hill a little way. I'm from Cleveland, but I've been here since I was little. We don't have a dad; it's just my mom and us," he pointed to himself and his brother, "and my two sisters, Sheela and

Stephanie. And you aren't a stranger. You're our neighbor."

The last few words caught Hubert up short. In New York, you could live next door to someone for twenty years and not know their name.

"It's nice to meet you boys. My name is Hubert Hastings. I moved here from New York. Do you know where that is?"

"Yes, sir. It's all the way across the United States. That's where the Statue of Liberty is. And where the Twin Towers that fell were. Did you see them fall?"

"I saw it on TV just like you did." He didn't want to tell them about being only a few blocks away from the devastation of that day. "Tell me, do you know where any good hiking trails are? I want to start slow because I've never hiked before."

"Sure do. The Woodland Trail is good. They have booklets that tell you what you're looking at. I've been on that trail a million times." Danny reached into his pocket and pulled out a pager. "Oh, oh, gotta get. Mom said she can't afford for me to have a phone like the other kids, but she got me this pager and pages me when she needs me to get home quick. See ya later, Mr. Hastings. Nice to meet you. Come on, Toby, I'll race you home."

Hubert watched the boys race away and noticed that Danny let Toby lead the way. Nice kid, he thought. And went to rake pine needles and pinecones from the front of his house.

* * *

Hubert traveled to Riverside. He had lunch at the famous Mission Inn, paid with cash, and thought over his plan one last time. Then, he visited Starbucks #1. He emailed the former head of Fox Accounting, now a senior partner in the combined firm. Then spent an hour at the local dog park, watching. He'd been thinking about getting a dog. He'd never had a pet, not even a goldfish.

Leaving the dog park, he visited Starbucks #2. He checked his email for a response. Nothing. He traveled to the Tyler Mall and window-shopped. After an hour and a half, he visited Starbucks #3.

Bingo. A bombastic email seared his computer screen. *"How dare you try to blackmail me! Who do you think you are? I'm contacting the police if you contact me again!"*

A smile lit Hubert's face. This was the reaction he expected. He typed a reply and waited. Within five minutes, he received an answer. He checked his offshore account and noted the large deposit.

While he drove, his thoughts raced. *Are you proud of yourself? Blackmail is a crime. Now you're a criminal.* Remembering a line from the T.V. show, *Bonanza,* Hubert could almost hear Ben Cartwright telling his sons, "Two wrongs don't make a right."

For several years, Hubert had suspected a few of Fox's largest clients were getting tax deductions they weren't entitled to. They were noted as things that wouldn't be questioned, but if one were familiar with the businesses involved and their prior returns, the expenses would have been picked up immediately. Those false entries gave the companies receiving them millions in tax deductions.

It was too late now; the 'big guy' had already made the first payment.

Though his conscience bothered him, Hubert was pleased that he'd figured out the 'creative accounting methods' and had sent proof of those findings to the cloud. He'd used different IP addresses for the emails to the senior partner. He knew the FBI or IRS could trace everything back to him, but he also knew the crooked senior partner wouldn't want anyone else involved. It was easier to pay the blackmail, at least for a time.

How do you make the already wrong action right, or at least more tolerable?

Swerving to miss a large rock that had tumbled down the mountainside, a thought cleared his already overloaded conscience. The next day, he again sent emails. This time to the two U.S. Senators from New York, the Securities and Exchange Commission, and the IRS. His conscience wouldn't let him not tell the authorities about some of Fox's sleazy accounting practices. He'd done his duty as a citizen and let the authorities deal with it as they saw fit.

Hubert spent hours on the phone with the offshore bank. He set up quarterly payments for all the employees that had over twenty years of service that had been let go. They would be sent out anonymously and would arrive a week before Thanksgiving.

With a clean conscience, Hubert felt more at ease than he had since he'd moved to the mountains. He decided to try out his new electric bike. He hadn't been on a bike since he was about sixteen, and riding it wasn't as easy as he'd remembered.

The bike had more power than expected, so he rode the deserted side streets near his cabin. Everything worked fine until he went too fast down the hill by his house. The front of the bike had a mind of its own and wobbled from side to side. Hubert, intent on trying to slow down, lost control of the steering. The bike pitched into a patch of gravel and did an end-over-end somersault.

Hubert sprawled half on the gravel and half on the pavement, gasping for breath. Luckily, he had on a helmet. He'd hit his head hard and lay there for a few minutes to catch his breath and move his extremities.

"Mr. Hastings! Are you okay?" Danny stood over him, eyes nearly popping from his head. "Does your foot hurt? It looks funny. I'm gonna get my mom. She's a nurse. She'll know what to do."

From his reclining position, Hubert watched Danny run to a nearby house. He pushed himself to a sitting position, but a searing pain shot from his ankle when he tried to stand. Something was terribly wrong.

Danny reappeared with a lovely-looking woman dressed in jeans and a plaid shirt—a touch of gray threaded through her strawberry-blond hair.

"Danny, please take this gentleman's bike to his house. She knelt by Hubert's side.

"Hi, I'm Helen. It looks like you did some damage to your ankle. I'm going to get my car and drive you to the ER. This needs to be X-rayed before we can tell if it's a bad sprain or if it's broken. Is that okay with you?"

He nodded.

"Do you have your ID and insurance information with you?" Hubert nodded again. "Okay, then. I'll get my car."

Helen saw him into the ER, where he received lots of extra attention because she'd brought him in; everyone at the hospital loved Helen. She told Hubert she had to pick up her girls and drive them home. But that she'd be back to get him.

After X-rays and a soft cast, Hubert waited in a wheelchair. A nurse pushed him through the ER doors when Helen drove up. He had crutches, a bag with his medication, and lots of paperwork.

Getting in the car was a task by itself. He wasn't sure how he'd be able to manipulate the five or six stairs to his deck. But with Helen's help, it was easier than he'd thought.

She made sure he was comfortable and elevated his foot. It was severely sprained and had a hairline fracture. Elevation and ice were required. Helen told him she or Danny would return and bring him an early dinner and some frozen peas for his ankle.

* * *

Thanksgiving was fast approaching, and Hubert's ankle hadn't healed as quickly as he wanted. However, he'd graduated from crutches to a scooter that he knelt on with his knee. It enabled him to get around on the ground floor, but his bedroom was upstairs. The stairs that Danny had said Mr. Asher had fallen or been pushed down.

Hubert got up and down the stairs on his butt, scooting one stair at a time. Upstairs, he had to use the dreaded crutches. And every time he teetered on the landing while trying to stand, he thought of Mr. Asher.

He couldn't have asked for a better neighbor than Helen and her four children. The first few weeks before he got the scooter, Helen had cooked him dinner every night. To pay her back, he insisted the kids come to his house after school and stay until she got home.

Hubert looked forward to their daily visits and even helped them with their homework. During the day, he grew weary of checking the stock market and continuously researching his holdings. Watching hours of commentary on daily news events set his teeth on edge. Especially when he saw the news report about Fox Accounting, an anonymous whistle-blower, and false tax documents, he turned to the cooking network.

He'd call himself a passable cook, even though for most of his life, he'd only cooked for himself and in her later years, his mother. When they'd had potlucks at work, everyone always ate what he brought and said it was delicious. Finally, he decided to take the plunge and make Thanksgiving dinner.

The weather had turned cold and rainy with a steady wind. TV's local weather channel called for snow on Thanksgiving Eve, with two feet predicted by Friday.

The phone felt strange in his hand. He rarely called anyone or received a call. "Hello, Helen, this is Hubert; how was your weekend?" He thought this sounded invasive of her privacy but didn't know what else to say.

"Hi, Hubert. It was great, thanks. It's funny you called. I was going to call you and invite you to join me and the kids for Thanksgiving dinner. Are you free?"

"Well, that's quite a coincidence. That's why I'm calling you. With all my free time, I've been watching lots of cooking shows, and I'd like to try my hand at making some of the recipes. And you and the kids have been so great at helping me since the accident.

I'd like to partially repay that kindness with a home-cooked meal. Besides, you work every day, and I just sit around. You deserve a day off. What do you say?"

She didn't answer right away, and his hopes plummeted. "Helen, are you still there?"
"Yes, I'm here, and we'd love to come to your house for Thanksgiving dinner. Thank you so much for the invite. What can we bring?"

"You just bring your nice self and the kids, of course. Oh, I know. Have the kids each write a short note they can read during dinner, telling everyone what they are thankful for."

Helen agreed and insisted on bringing the table decorations the kids had been working on, including the centerpiece. Hubert smiled as he hung up the phone. This was nice; somehow, he felt less like a loose end or an afterthought. He put another log on the fire and sat down to make his menu and shopping list. Then he went in search of his mother's dishes.

DOWNHILL

Karene Horst

Deep breaths. In. Out. You can do this. Her chest hardly moved as her eyes locked onto the tips of her skis, the rounded ends soaring over the dark green treetops that pointed up at her like spear tips. The chairlift whirred along before it jolted to a halt. Sara gripped the restraint bar while the chair swayed and bounced. She gulped.

Deep breaths. In. Out. You got this.

Sara had learned to ski ages ago as a twelve-year-old, catapulting across the bunny slopes and beginner zones at Mammoth on the last vacation she tagged along with her father and his new wife. Just like riding a bike, her friends teased her almost two decades later. They talked her into this ski weekend in the mountains closer to Los Angeles. Big Bear.

"Do they really have bears?" Sara almost whispered, her eyes widening with slight alarm.

They all laughed at her. They pressed her into joining them for a girls-only, three-day getaway in the snow, no excuses.

Susan bailed first. Her fiancé insisted she join him for a family gathering.

"A must," she rolled her eyes. "An 'absolute deal-breaker with Mom'."

Candace flashed a knowing smirk as if to say, *it's only gonna get worse if you let Mommy start calling the shots,* but said nothing.

Then Candace caught the flu, apologizing for abandoning the expedition with little more than a croaking sound. Once she flaked, Teresa seesawed before sending a last minute text that her boss demanded she attend a weekend work session. Too late to get the room deposit back or the lift tickets refunded. Sara headed up solo, packing her two-wheel-drive Honda Civic with mismatched winter gear on loan from Susan and a brand-new pair of snow chains she had no idea how to install. Her girlfriends all agreed they would not expect her to pay their share because they canceled, so Sara would have the cabin with the teddy-bear-themed decor that slept four all to herself at no extra cost. She could not let everyone's hard-earned money go to waste.

"It'll be fun," she reassured herself.

She nibbled on the memories of her family ski trip. Her father even complimented her on mastering this challenging skill. She would never forget the sensation that embraced her when his admiring expression united with her exhilaration at discovering how to fly across snow.

But at that moment she did not feel the fun. She felt terror. She should have taken a refresher course. Signing up for a group lesson might have allowed her to swish down the mountain with a seasoned instructor to minimize risk. But the company passed her up for that promotion and the price tag of a lesson would sink her already listing budget. So she decided to act unafraid. Take a chance. She remembered how she grinned nonstop during the Mammoth trip. One of her few fond childhood memories. Just like riding a bike.

The rocking motion of the chair lessened until it hung still, even in the brittle wind that ruffled the fake fur on one of Sara's gloves. Her chest hurt as she sucked in the cold air.

How long will the chair stop here?

Would she get stuck, stranded in the sky above the pine-needled trees? Sara peered from her high perch at the skiers and snowboarders below crisscrossing the cascading bands of white flanked by thick groves of trees and boulders. The screech of their edges scraping across the icy patches echoed. They executed their rhythmic banking motions with a choreographed precision and beauty. To Sara, their maneuvers appeared effortless.

Her head throbbed. To limit altitude sickness, she had drunk so much water on the drive up and before wriggling under the covers to sleep that she was awake most of the night peeing in the cabin's tiny closet of a bathroom. But had altitude AND nerves conspired to roil her stomach and buffet her skull? As she contemplated whether or not to release the balloon of panic billowing against her gut, she reminded herself that they had to stop the chairlift when some moron fell either getting on or off the lift. After a minute or so more, the machinery clicked and grated and the chair lurched into motion. She relaxed her grip on the bar a few seconds before realizing that meant she must confront the ultimate test for any novice skier—getting off the lift without crashing.

Of course she would crash. She had already crashed – a spectacular train wreck. As she attempted to sashay toward the loading spot to wait for the chair to scoop her up from behind, she immediately planted her pole in a deep pile of slush, slipped sideways, crossed the right ski over her left tip as she tilted too far to the left, then plummeted to the ground landing in a heap. The metal chair whacked her helmet as it passed overhead. A loud buzzer rang out as the chairlift jerked and shuddered to a halt. The mishap tweaked her knee, making her wince, but the damage to her ego far exceeded any to her body. The hefty chairlift operator behind the mirror glasses swiftly grabbed her under an arm and by the seat of her snow pants before settling her upright and in place again.

"Everything alright?" he asked in a nonjudgmental tone.

She nodded her head quickly, too shocked to consider that maybe she should not take that lift. Amidst the low-key mumbling and assorted groans, a voice rang out, "Go back to Orange County."

As a twelve-year-old she had never fallen while hopping on the chairlift. Getting off the lift she had repeatedly tangled herself into a mess, until by day three she scooted away from the slow moving bench like a pro.

Approaching the top of the lift this time, she signaled to the operator to decelerate the chair as it neared the end of her ride, exactly as her Mammoth ski instructor taught her. She reached out her gloved hand and pumped it up and down. Ensconced in the warm booth, the lift operator hunkered behind the window enveloped in a hooded jacket. She could not see a face, only opaque black sunglasses. The chair cruised along at its steady pace. Probably stoned or hungover, Sara moaned to herself.

She planted her skis almost two feet apart on the slick surface as soon as the chair reached the hardpacked mound of snow at the end of the lift. She had seconds to stand and glide away before the chair would rapidly swing 180 degrees for the return trip to ferry more bodies up the mountain. Sara grasped her poles, one in each hand, commanded her torso to straighten upright, and slid a few yards before veering haphazardly into a snowbank to avoid plowing through a trio of snowboarders huddled in the middle of the chairlift off-ramp. A more experienced skier would have maneuvered around them and any other obstacle presenting itself. Sara could muster the bare minimum of control. At least she had not collided with anyone. The chair operator did not even have to stop the lift or rescue her. A small accomplishment, Sara reminded herself. That's what the THINK POSITIVE podcaster recommended. Measure your life in small achievements, kudos to yourself when things don't go too wrong.

Sara tried to sing along with that encouraging refrain, but sometimes she just wanted to scream "SHUT UP." Not today. For now she would relish her tiny victories with a weak smile.

She managed to get her skis, poles, and the rest of her body in an upright and forward-moving position without too much drama. She planted her poles and propelled herself away from the lift. Smooth, relatively flat terrain enticed her to advance. A handful of skiers sailed past her. Through the sparse trees on her left she could see a hillside crowded with skiers and snowboarders careening downhill or traversing the sheer slope. She cringed at the rasping noise created by their snowboards or skis carving through the icy crust coating the hillside. Sara commended herself for not choosing that run. The section she had wandered onto bolstered her courage as she gained momentum, alternating her pole strokes to guide herself along. She caught an edge but quickly righted herself. *OK. Good job. Small successes.* Yes, everyone else expertly whooshed by her. But she had not fallen or banged into anyone.

Great job!

Her stomach dropped as her skis rode up a small rise. She feared she would lose her balance, but instead, she glided over it and even picked up speed on the downside while maintaining her stance. *Cool!* She took a deep breath and congratulated herself once again.

You can do this.

The excitement and joy she experienced learning to ski at Mammoth bubbled up inside her.

Her skis bounced and drifted slightly across the hardpacked snow but never crossed. She sliced through the occasional loose slush shaved off the frozen surface by other pairs of skis or snowboards. No problem. She smiled. She snowplowed, pointing her skis slightly toward each other to slow herself, then straightened them to go faster. She stopped a few times to test her brakes. She graduated to clumsy but effective turns, putting all of her weight on one ski as she leaned in one direction then the other.

OK, shaky and scary but OK.

Her eyes bugged out as the slant of the hill increased, but she coasted to the more level segment without a hitch.

She had soldered her attention to the space immediately in front of her tips, examining not much more than ten to twenty feet beyond. As her confidence grew, she expanded her focus and glanced around at the pine trees, at the spectacular view. She gazed at the mountain tops across the valley. Then she noticed a gathering of skiers and boarders. Suddenly she realized her ski tips steered toward a horizon on the smooth, bland slope that swept her along. A cliff. A cluster of snowboarders sat on the edge near an outcropping of trees, their feet fastened onto their boards in a wide stance. They slumped forward with their heads dipped as if studying the ground far below. A pair of skiers stood at the edge, staring downward before they plunged out of sight.

Suddenly she spotted the trail sign with the black diamond next to the name MIRACLE MILE. Staked to the right of the sign, a black banner rippling in the wind declared that run MOST DIFFICULT. In a snowbank farther to the left she saw a fluttering blue banner with the words MORE DIFFICULT. The blue portion of the signpost read HOG BACK next to a blue square with a left arrow. She knew which fork in the road she would take. But still, Sara panicked. *Wasn't this a green?* She thought she was on Summit Run. The sign should have sported a green round circle, like a happy face.

She snowplowed to a stop, her legs spread wide and toes directed inward, her kneecaps facing each other. She struggled to swivel her legs and slide her skis together without falling. She planted her poles next to her skis as deep as she could before pulling off her right glove so she could dig into her coat pocket for her cell phone. Her poles wobbled before cascading to the ground. One clattered to a rest on top of her skis.

She studied the trail map she had stored on her phone as fear crawled up her spine and crept across her neck and shoulders. She had chosen to ride the East Mountain Express because it would deliver her to the top of Summit Run, an easy green for beginners. But she had made a wrong turn after tumbling off the lift, lured away by the long, flat stretch that fed into Miracle Mile. While navigating the mild upper section, she had mistaken the run she saw to the left of her as the harder way. Nope. The slope she had balked at earlier, the almost vertical one teeming with skis and poles and snowboards and bodies, that was the easy way.

Sara practically toppled over in the process of collecting her poles. She pushed herself away from Miracle Mile toward the ridge overhanging Hog Back. She grimaced in horror. The terrain below her did not look anymore painless than the MOST DIFFICULT Miracle Mile, but it gradually flowed into a gentle incline before curving into Summit Run. Skiers and snowboarders floated across the snow, some with amazing grace, others with jerking motions that sometimes ended in disaster.

A lone skier dashed past her, so close the displaced air blasted her as he barreled by. She flinched at the burst of chatter from his skis hurtling over the corduroy, the rigid grooves left behind by last night's grooming.

She stood motionless—her shocked expression glued onto the path below her. She gasped short breaths. Her chest hurt. Her head pounded. She pictured herself flailing out of control, smacking into a tree guarding the border of the run, or slamming onto the snow in a face-plant, her arms and legs thrashing before knotting into unnatural positions, her poles flung askew above her, a lone ski racing toward the bottom until a brake could catch and arrest its descent. She applauded herself for splurging on the extra cash to insure her ski equipment from damage due to an accident.

She could take the coward's way out. Unclip her boots from her bindings and sidestep down the worst part of Hog Back before reaching the lower, less terrifying Summit Run.

How many feet would she have to descend? A thousand? Two? She had difficulty judging distances. Even this minor section, so minuscule on the map, spread before her like an impossibility. A sudden gust of wind surprised her and threw her to the ground.

She wiped away a tear. Then another. They left sharp smears of pain across her cheeks as the moisture paved pathways for the wind to seep deeper and leave behind its harsh chill. She gulped away a sob. Then everything gurgled up and spilled out. Her father's indifference, her mother's diagnosis, her failed job interview, the boyfriend who never called her back. She couldn't even count on her friends.

She indulged in a good long cry, pouring out her misery to the unrelenting wind, the stoic mountains towering around her, the pine trees reaching away from her toward the sky.

"There's never an easy way," she wailed. She did not feel like meditating on her affirmative mantras or engaging in positive self-talk or any of that other nonsense. She was stuck. Frozen to this hillside.

"You alright?"

The high-pitched voice stunned Sara. She dragged her gloved hand across her face and angled her head away.

"I'm fine. Just resting."

"Good place for a break. Mind if I join?" the girl asked.

Without waiting for Sara to respond, she hopped on her snowboard closer to Sara before plopping backward onto the seat of her purple polka-dotted snow pants. Her pink-and-violet-striped helmet had a silver unicorn horn strapped above her rainbow mirrored goggles.

The child proceeded to babble without pause–how much she loved her new Burton board, she was sad her dog Rascal had to stay home, she could not wait for tomorrow as her mother had promised they would rent a movie and eat popcorn after dinner, and on and on until Sara, exhausted from trying to keep up with the monologue, interrupted her.

"Are you snowboarding alone? Where's your family?"

"Oh, Dad used to ski but he says his knees bother him, and Mom needed a day off. My older brother Trey is boarding with his friends at the freestyle park. He's into rails and aerials."

"So … they let you snowboard on your own, by yourself?"

Sara studied the girl's small frame. She could not have been more than nine or ten.

"Well, it's not like I'm out here alone." The girl gestured toward a trio of skiers whizzing by. "I carry my cell phone and I've got ski patrol on speed dial. Besides, my dad says I learned to snowboard before I learned to walk. We have a cabin up here so we come up every weekend. Trey's supposed to watch out for me, but I get bored with the park. I'm not into tricks or epic wipeouts–I'd rather shred. He doesn't notice when I take off on my own." She shrugged her tiny shoulders. "Besides, I can take care of myself," she said in a confident tone that reminded Sara of a little girl she knew ages ago.

"So anyway, I'm all rested and my rear end's freezing."

In a fluid motion, the girl jumped up from her seated position into standing on her board and slid away, tossing her hand in Sara's direction. "See ya."

A wry smile played across Sara's lips as she reviewed her goals for the day. *Goal Number One: Don't run into anyone.*

She clambered to her feet, swaying dangerously to one side before she snapped her legs straight, cementing them above each ski. She poled herself closer to the upper lip of Hog Back, her legs moving stiffly in a skating motion. She focused on the hillside beneath her curlicued with the tracks of previous visitors.

She inhaled the alpine view along with the brisk winter air. The blue water of Big Bear Lake twinkled in the sunshine. She thrust her chest forward as she shoved off with her poles, both ski tips aiming downhill.

MY COWBOY,
NOT MY COWBOY
Lori Brookes

He had me at, "I've got enough portable electric fence to build a two-acre corral." At the very least that grabbed both my attention and curiosity. I mean, who owns enough portable electric fencing to create two acres of safe space for their horse while out wandering the country? My cowboy does! He technically isn't a cowboy. That title is a misnomer when crossing the path of any wide-brimmed hat, boots, and chaps-wearing man saddled atop a horse.

I have stood corrected. To be addressed as a cowboy you need some cows. Makes total sense.
So this cowboy, with his portable electric fence, is more definitively categorized as a horseman. His name… Carson. He is a renowned specialist in founder (a horse hoof disease) prevention and rehabilitation.

Oddly, we met online, but not in the way you may think. Not through an online dating kind of thing, but via a Facebook Group page—the Wind River Range group. I joined the group's page after I returned from an epic backpacking trip to the Wind River Range in Wyoming. I belonged to a women's hiking network that spanned the entire U.S. and I happened to see a post about this backpacking trip through a part of our country I hadn't seen. I was intrigued and signed up!

My solo road trip–and by now there had been many–started in Big Bear. I met up with these gals off of a sketchy dirt road, and I say sketchy as I was driving a front-wheel drive Honda HRV named Red. We went down many roads together that she wasn't built for, but she had grit—just like her driver! As usual, I was the oldest in the bunch, having started my hiking career at age 59, and in typical form, I didn't make a big deal about it. I found that I could hike with both the best and youngest.

We trekked for three days and made our camp along the "S" turns of the Green River Lakes. Given my age, it wasn't far-fetched to hear the music of CC&R playing in my mind, one of my early teen favorites. Insert air guitar here!

What an amazing place. So different from the landscape of California, even at our respectable 7,000 feet elevation in Big Bear. We just don't have this kind of green. Lush and blanketing everything. Happily, we also don't have mosquitoes the size of miniature helicopters that gargle with Deet and spit it out in our faces while laughing out loud at our attempt to … not be eaten alive. There is a certain price you pay for those shades of green.

Back to my cowboy, not my cowboy, who turned out to be from these parts. I returned home with some excellent shots from my campsite overlooking not only the Green River Lakes and surrounding magnificence, but also the monumental-sized presence of Squaretop Mountain towering in the background. As I do, I shared photos from my trip on Facebook with friends and also on the Wind River Range Group page. The administrator of the group reached out to ask if they could use one of my photographs for their page's cover photo and of course, I said yes.

It was that image that spurred Carson to open a chat in Messenger and that exchange was our first official online encounter.

After I performed my due diligence vetting process for online strangers, I determined that he was probably an okay guy, and I responded in kind. That began our conversation, one that in short order went from text to chat. He was educated, intelligent, and worldly. An avid reader of high-level and thought-provoking books. I'm a sucker for a man who can hold his own in a conversation with any sort of depth. No sports talk for me! I learned a bit about his life as a wanderer. Never married or saddled by anyone other than his horse and dog. His education took him down a road of finance, but he opted out, and outside … a life of endless adventures and roaming … from river guiding in Alaska to snow ski instructing in the North, to speaking engagements at universities on his current tradecraft. A fascinating life, especially for someone like me who lived the second act as a long-term married woman with two kids, two dogs, a cat, a home in suburbia, and a corporate banking job. Now divorced and living the third act of my life somewhat wild and fancy-free.

After eighteen months of frequent calls and long conversations, and into and out of the global pandemic, I told Carson I was taking a solo road trip toward his neck of the woods from mine, and wondered if in his travels we might cross paths. We had a close encounter, but our meanderings did not magically align like the stars.

It would be another two years before we would finally meet in person. I tried to get Carson to come up to our beautiful mountain town. However, with prohibitive California gas and diesel prices, the exorbitant price for hay, and limited open spaces with grassland, he just wasn't interested. Consequently, I went his way instead, after all, I had to see that fencing!

This time I drove from Big Bear to Sedona, Rimrock to be precise, just outside of Sedona. Carson had found a beautiful spot-on federal grassland to camp with his horse Bohemian (Bo for short), and his little but mighty dog, Rick. His nickname is The Ranger, and he even sports a badge on his dog vest. Carson often writes witty tales of Rick warning off coyotes and protecting their temporary residences across the country they roam. This is home to them. There is no other. No brick and mortar, no lath and plaster, just wherever they land and plant some stakes. Or at the very least, portable electric fencing.

Concern came from friends about meeting up with a man I had never met, out in the middle of nowhere. This caring was not lost on me. I always have a Plan B, C, or D. My intuition operates at a higher level when I travel and becomes even more fine-tuned when I travel solo. I told the caring and concerned that when I got there, if I felt any sense of something off, I'd be out of there. I camp/sleep in my Jeep and just like at home, my escape route is down pat. In the Jeep, however, this does require some yoga-type moves to get from the back to the driver's seat, but hey that's part of what keeps me young and fit.

Arrived! A big puff of dirt settled behind 'Lil Grey, my Jeep, and admittedly I felt a little something-

something tumbling about in my stomach. Something off? First meeting jitters? Time will tell. The first greeter, of course, was Rick, The Ranger. I saw Bo in his corral as I peeked around the very large combo 5th wheel/horse trailer. Carson's home on wheels. I'm barely here and it's already a course in fascination.

Carson's cadence on approach was contemplatively slow, as you might imagine it would be for someone who does not live in the hustle and bustle of life as we know it. Even with a slower life in the mountains of Big Bear, compared to city life, it is still not as slow as life on an open road. No schedules per se, except the feeding kind, and life is about whatever comes your way. Like me! Now he had to deal with me. Calendar me into the mix.

We exchanged a friendly, easy, and uncomplicated greeting, like "Hey I know you!" Followed by a mutual hug. Carson then helped me set up my tent extension attached to 'Lil Grey. Ranger Rick tried to help but, you know what, he was all paws.

All set up, it's time for the home-on-the-range tour, and you must have guessed that my priority was to see Bo and his fenced-off acreage. Bo was a beautiful draft horse. He is a rescue, as is Rick. They are the cutest roaming family I have ever met. They are the only roaming family I have ever met.

As promised, there was the electric fencing all set up for Bo's protection, with some delicious wild grasses at his whim, and enough room to feel what it must be like for a horse in the wild. Mostly. The fencing is unobtrusive, with skinny stakes wired together producing an electrical current to deter the larger wild things from getting in or Bo from getting out. And let's not forget about Rick who roams and protects the perimeter.

Carson invited me over to meet another roaming cowboy friend, who was traveling with his two ponies. Turned out they had serendipitously met somewhere weeks earlier and that's how Carson came to know about these amazing grasslands in Rimrock.

The next scene was right out of a Robert Redford movie. There's me, the now mountain girl, in her best cowboy boots (Carson told me to bring them), Carson's cowboy friend Ryder from Ohio, Carson, The

Ranger, and the local farrier putting new shoes on Ryder's ponies, Silver and Rowdy. I'm the only human present not wearing chaps! And let me just say something about chaps, as I watched this scene unfold, standing behind three "cowboys" all very engaged in the horseshoeing event… I say to myself, "Nice asses!"

Up until now, I hadn't seen Carson without his 'cowboy' hat on, I had no idea what was going on under there. I had seen his strong square jawline. I think he had blue eyes and the fringe of his hair looked to be gray. He stood 5-9" to 5-10" and was quite handsome. His hat finally came off so he could scratch his head, the thinking kind of scratch, and there it was… a full head of thick gray hair flopped out with a little Elvis-like curl bouncing on his forehead. I sensed he had little to no idea about his appeal. I'm a bit cowboy-struck, even though he wasn't a cowboy by definition.

At suppertime, Carson invited me inside his man cave, to have my meal. We each prepped our food, mine a little on the gourmet side and his—out of a can. I offered him some of my marinated tri tip, originally he declined but once his senses were engaged, he took a stab. Seeing how The Ranger was the official dishwasher, I was glad I'd brought my plate and silverware. I'm a hard 'NO' on that! Not sure if soap and hot water were ever involved after I left for my tent, but y'all do yours, and I'll do mine.

After dinner I had more of an opportunity to take a visual tour of the man cave, finding the RV portion of the trailer space to be quite small. I counted at least eight 'cowboy" hats', some were poised up on the bed, a few mounted on the ceiling, with a couple more in the dining area. Hats and books … the epitome of a bibliophile roaming 'cowboy' bachelor pad.

I spent a few days with Carson exploring the surrounding area on foot. His friend Ryder offered me to ride Silver, the easier of his two ponies, and we all took off on horseback to the edge of a nearby gorge. We parked the horses and hiked down into the gorge to see enormous red rock walls filled with petroglyphs. They both poked fun at my footwear, the cowboy boots Carson told me to bring for riding. I didn't know we were going rock scrambling or I'd have brought a change of boots on the ride. And it didn't stop there, "Where's your chaps?" they chided. Good thing I've got thick skin.

I felt my visit with Carson was somewhat awkward for him. Maybe it was me or maybe it was just having someone, anyone, in his space for more than a few hours. I'll never know. I didn't ask.

Ranger Rick loved me though! Dogs are so much less complicated. He would be at my tent each morning and at the end of each day, to greet me and conversely to say goodnight. I'd let him in and give him some treats, then he'd go back to his portion of the man cave, which truthfully was all of it. Carson's sidekick, his best friend. What a sweetie! The day I left Rimrock, about 100 miles down the road, I got a text from Carson that read, "Bo and Rick already miss you."

Not my cowboy…

* * *

I befriended Ryder on that trip, and we exchanged numbers. "Let's keep in touch." In our brief talks, I learned that our lives had many similarities, in that we both had been married, raised children, and had grandchildren. Even though he was a roamer, it was only for a few months each year when the weather in Ohio turned cold. He'd set out with his ponies for the warmth and wonder found in the Southwest. Dissimilar were our former ways of life—he had been a cattle rancher, a cowboy, (finally, I can use that term legitimately), and I had led a corporate turned entrepreneur life, dwelling in the city. He hand-built his home from the timber, flora, and fauna on his land, with his nearest neighbor some five miles away. Yet, we were similar in our committed lives to other people and children, and this became our common ground for life experience conversations and ways of being.

Ryder was a delight! Handsome, joyful, fun, well-traveled with an infectious laugh. He was in many respects more of an adventurous type. Like me! My introduction to adventure came after a dedicated life to others and where greener pastures waited. I joyfully discovered in my post-marriage life that I don't have to do anything more than what I wanted to do, and I could go anywhere I wanted! I think the same things held true for Ryder.

His flexibility and genuine interest in adventuring with me brought him to Big Bear, at my invitation, to explore my neck of the woods before it got too cold. I found a friend on the East side of town with a chunk of land that could accommodate a traveling cowboy and his ponies. We took to the wild, off the beaten familiar trails that I knew intimately on foot and offroading. I knew Ryder's Southwest adventures included some amazing sites, geological delights, riding through rivers, the presence of authentic petroglyphs, ancient dinosaur bones, hiking and riding through slot canyons, and playgrounds of sheer-walled red rock gorges. I wanted to show him some equally interesting things that existed on our mountain.

Our first stop was a ride to nearby "Eye of God," the giant white quartz outcropping revered by the indigenous people of Big Bear Valley, the Serranos—"people of the pines." The outcropping must have been awe-inspiring before it was blown up by gold miners and horrendously reduced in size, only to discover there was no gold. That was a common theme up here. Blow it up, find no gold, abandon.

Through disease brought by the white invaders, their numbers were drastically reduced, and were displaced by the invasion. A way too common human horror story in the United States, and Big Bear owns plenty of chapters in that book. The quartz mound is still beautiful and remains sacred despite its unfortunate past. We spent some time here soaking in the magic of the mound.

The foothills in both Baldwin Lake and Lake Erwin are etched by forest service roads, cultivated hiking trails, and desire paths (also known as game or use trails). The latter is carved by local livestock, the deer population, and our beloved wild burros. I had high hopes of crossing paths with those furry beings! I just love them. I was also a little curious about the reaction from Ryder's ponies, Silver and Rowdy, as long as they didn't spook and leave me tumbling to the ground. Sadly, it was a no-burro day.

Deadman's Ridge was next on our self-guided tour. We headed slowly and respectfully into sacred native burial ground territory, flanked by both the fated ridge and a seasonal creek. Local historical lore tells the legend of this area where a forged road led to the Rose Mine, through Lake Erwin. It was a gold mine. There was another road that could reach the mine, but this particular road was closer for delivering supplies from town to the mining area, however, it went through the sacred burial site of the Serranos. Warned by the native people not to take this route, the land baron ignored the warning and sent his worker, of Mexican descent, not bothering to tell him of the warning. Saddled with food supplies for the mining community, he set out on horseback, only to be killed in transit by the native people. They dragged his body up to the top of the ridge that overlooks the burial ground and left his corpse there as a warning. Hence the name, *Deadman's Ridge.*

We stopped in the now-dry seasonal creek, juxtaposed to the stone grave markers, and took a quiet moment off the ponies to contemplate the area, the bloody history, and the surprising serenity of it all. Wild burros brayed briefly in the distance, the wind fluffed the rabbit brush and rose sage, the peace and ultimate quiet—as we paid homage to the ancestors of this valley.

We covered quite a bit of ground, Ryder, the ponies, and me. Riding side-by-side, we swapped more life stories… where we've been and where we'd each like to go next. Since Joshua Tree was so close, Ryder thought he might like to explore that vast desert land. That spurred me to ask him if he had ever explored Death Valley, as my mind already had us riding together through our largest national park in the Lower 48, my most visited and favorite of our national parks. He'd not been! I'd love to introduce him to Death Valley, and on horseback. Well, how exciting would that be?

Our ride seemed a slow gait back to camp, with a contemplative pause in our previous free-flowing conversation. The ponies came to an unsolicited stop, and Ryder reached out to me with his rawhide gloved hand, which I accepted and placed my hand in his. It felt like a chapter torn right out of a whisk-me-away romantic novel.

There was an awkward pause before he uttered these words through his asymmetric smirking smile, "Take me to Death Valley."

The next day our mountain visit was nearing its end. While Ryder packed up camp, I had my final visit with the ponies.

"Here she comes again with those apples!"

The apples from Big Bear were in abundance this year and they loved their sweet treats from me! With Rowdy and Silver the last to load, we said our final goodbye with a longer-than-usual hug and a kiss.

About 150 miles down the road I received a text from Ryder that read, "I miss you already, and the ponies miss your apples!"

My cowboy…

ONE, ONE THOUSAND, TWO, ONE THOUSAND

Christie Walker Bos

A light sheen of perspiration dots my forehead with the realization that there is something wrong with the plane. For a full ten seconds, I'm the only passenger who knows we will not be taking off. How do I know? I count.

Earlier, sitting on the runway, the jet engines had roared to life in anticipation of takeoff, the brakes fighting to hold the plane in place. With a slight jolt, the plane rushed forward, starting its race down the runway. That's when I started counting … one, one thousand; two, one thousand.

* * *

This counting-during-takeoff routine started fifty years ago when, as an eager, sparkly-eyed intern for the L.A. Times, I wandered among the passengers assembled in an empty hanger looking for someone to interview. Their trip to Hawaii had been interrupted when their airplane failed to lift off, coming to a screeching halt at the end of the runway. No one had been injured, and although the experience rattled people, the most prevalent complaint had been the disruption of their vacation plans.

As a twenty-year-old female reporter in the '70s, I always felt an unspoken pressure to prove to my male colleagues and editors that I had what it takes to cover hard news such as plane crashes, wildfires, and crime scenes. Back in the day, female journalists were often given safe, soft news feature stories. It didn't help that I hailed from Big Bear, a small town in the San Bernardino mountains, or that my two-year degree came from a local community college. Still, the quality of my writing proved to be the key that opened the door and landed me an internship despite my lowly pedigree.

When the editor called to tell me, I'd beat out the other applicants, I guess I sounded shocked. Then he said something I've never forgotten. "A degree from a fancy four-year college doesn't mean a thing if you can't write your way out of a box." I later learned that he had worked his way up from the mailroom to the editor with only a high school diploma, so there was that.

For the six months that I worked at the Times, I was the only female reporter covering hard news. The guys in the press room—and they were all guys, many of them old enough to be my father—took me under their collective wings like they would their daughter, vacillating between being overprotective to cajoling me to get out there and take risks.

Growing up in Big Bear provided me with skills not usually associated with young women from the city. Because, when you live in the mountains you have to be prepared for anything. I always carried snow chains, hiking boots, a daypack filled with survivor gear, and water bottles in the trunk of my car … even in the city. Assigned to cover a brush fire near Griffith Park, I arrived at the scene, changed into hiking boots, slipped on my pack, and took to the trails until I found a fire crew to interview, passing out water from my daypack before I left.

Another time, I'd been assigned a story in Wrightwood. A snowstorm had swept in, and the Highway Patrol closed the road. No one could travel beyond the roadblock unless they had chains, which I did. And much to the amazement of the officers manning the roadblock, I strapped the chains on the rear tires myself—something my dad insisted I learn the day I received my driver's license. After that, the guys in the press room nicknamed me Mountain Girl, a name I accepted with a twinge of pride. If a story came in that involved trekking through mud, hiking through brush, or driving on snowy roads, I'd inevitably hear someone suggest, "Give it to Mountain Girl."

Being assigned to a plane crash, where I only had to brave the freeways on the way to the airport, seemed like a step in the right direction until I learned that a) no one else was available, and b) the plane hadn't actually crashed, more like failed to take off.

I knew I needed to find a unique angle that would make my story stand out and maybe, just maybe, earn me a little respect for my writing ability not just my Mountain Girl moxie. A ticker tape of possible headlines scrolled through my mind, each one more mundane than the next: Plane Fails to Takeoff; No Injuries During Failed Takeoff; Plane Crashes at LAX, No Injuries.

As I walked past a family wearing matching Hawaiian shirts, I overheard someone in the crowd say, "I knew we were in trouble. I knew we were going to crash."

My head whipped around so fast that I almost gave myself whiplash. Who said that?

When a woman's voice asked, "How did you know?" I homed in on the conversation like a shark on a blood scent.

The "clairvoyant," a man about my father's age wearing khaki shorts, sandals, and of course, a Hawaiian shirt, explained to a young mother, holding a baby, "Because I count the ground run."

Was this guy an off-duty pilot?

As if reading my mind, the woman asked, "Are you a pilot?"

"Retired."

I joined the conversation by introducing myself. "Christina Worster, Los Angeles Times. Can you explain what you mean by counting the ground run? How does that work?"
In a calm, steady voice that belied the fact that an hour ago, this man had exited a plane using the evacuation slide, the ex-pilot explained.

"Every twin-engine commercial aircraft's takeoff lasts around 30 to 35 seconds, from throttle up to wheels off the ground, regardless of the size or the load of the aircraft. When the pilot releases the brakes, I start counting, one, one thousand; two, one thousand. When I hit forty, I knew we had a problem."

While I had my headline, the one that ended up securing my career as a journalist—*Passenger Knew the Plane Would Crash*—I also had a new ritual to perform every time I flew.

* * *

Once you know a thing, you can't unknow it. Ever since the interview with the retired pilot, I count during takeoff. This, however, is the first time the plane has failed to leave the ground.

I'm at forty-five, one thousand in my count and we're still not airborne. Holding my breath, I await the announcement that doesn't come. The squeal of brakes elicits cries of panic from the other passengers as the plane shudders, fighting its forward momentum.

Next to me sits an elderly couple … probably my age … who look terrified. The husband takes his wife's hand, and they begin to pray together in soft murmurs.

For some reason, I'm weirdly calm. Maybe it's because I've had several seconds of pre-knowledge of our predicament to get used to the idea that the plane will not be leaving the ground. Or maybe it's because fifty years ago, the pilot of that flight heading to Hawaii brought the plane to a stop with no injuries, so I figure this pilot will do the same.

The sound of ripping metal draws my attention to the window. The plane broke through the chain link fence at the end of the runway. A portion of fencing catches on the wing and is dragged like a piece of toilet paper stuck to a shoe. We come to a bumpy stop in a weedy field filled with tall stalks of yellow mustard flowers. The cabin erupts in a cacophony of sounds as passengers cheer, cry, and breathe audible sighs of relief. The couple next to me unclenched their hands before crossing themselves and whispering, "Thank you, Jesus."

There are several reasons why a plane fails to lift off. At this point, since no one knows exactly what's happened, the situation is treated as an all-out emergency. Passengers leave everything behind as they exit quickly via the emergency slides. Fire trucks and ambulances arrive on scene triggering media alerts. Buses are deployed to transport passengers to a safe location where medical care, blankets, and bottles of water are provided.

As I'm standing in a hanger large enough for a 747, surrounded by my fellow passengers, the press is ushered inside, prompting a powerful sense of dèjá vu. I watch as reporters and photographers weave in and out of the crowd like wolves tracking their prey, sniffing out the perfect subject.

I spot a young reporter scanning the crowd. Tall, and thin, her head on a swivel, she searches for the interviewee who will give her that unique perspective.

I walk over. "Who do you work for?"

"The Chronicle," she answers, as she looks me up and down, quickly deciding I'm not who she wants to interview.

Having been in her shoes, I can guess what she's thinking. There has got to be someone better than this gray-haired granny. Maybe if I'd been injured or had my head bandaged or I'd been strapped to a gurney I might have made an interesting subject. But looking uninjured, she decides I'm not the subject who will give her an award-winning story.

She's wrong, I think with a sly smile, knowing I'm about to make her day, maybe even give her career a lift, much like mine had been boosted years ago.

I touch her arm gently, lean in, and say in a conspiratorial whisper, "I knew the plane was going to crash."

Now I have her attention. "How?"

"I count. One, one thousand. Two, one thousand."

COYOTE DAY

Karene Horst

He sniffed and flicked his tongue at the trickle of blood dripping from his left hind leg. Some of the syrupy liquid splattered red streaks onto the snow shoring up the scraggly mountain mahogany. His fur, wet from his blood and saliva, matted against his thigh. He lifted his head, alerted to a sound he could not place. A squirrel scurrying along an icy bough? A clump of snow falling off a branch? He did not know. The coyote did know he must watch for the big one, the leader who nipped him as he tried to slink back into the den with the rest of the pack earlier that day when they returned from a hunt. He had hoped the leader would have forgotten why he had chased him off the day before. But the big one hadn't forgotten and reminded the younger coyote with a vicious snarl and a gaping tear in the meaty part of his left hindquarter. Reminded him that nothing was forgotten.

He limped along a winding trail through a patch of manzanita over the hardpacked snow, a narrow path pounded into a more solid surface by a succession of heavy boots and paw prints. The boot tracks belonged to humans, obviously. He sniffed at the paw prints. Just dogs. Several. Some large, some only a bit smaller than him. Then he followed his nose to a slick green sack knotted closed at the top. A foul odor wafted from the animal droppings smooshed inside the plastic baggy. He also detected the slight scent of a human as well. He snorted, clearing his head and nostrils of the leavings.

A starving coyote might have torn into the bag in a feeble attempt to find anything edible concealed within the muck. But he was not starving, not yet. He ate yesterday afternoon before the big one ran him off. A vole had slipped out of its underground nest in pursuit of a stray seed or tidbit to nibble when the sun shone brightest and warmest. He surprised the rodent as it scurried back home, clamping his jaws around the vole's backside and sinking his teeth into its soft underside.

The coyote's hunger, ever present and engulfing, cinched his stare to some movement in the withered undergrowth bracing a dead tree stump. The wind maybe? It riffled through the grayish beige hairs on his chest and the tan and black fur on his back. He twitched his ears, waiting to hear if the movement might signify his meal. A rustling from some neighboring bushes. He froze. He studied his pathway to the low stand of yellowed stalks and gnarled shrubs. Thinning snow and frost-tipped dead weeds surrounded the dense thicket. Anything escaping would have to dash through a well-lit backdrop of unprotected landscape unless it could flee into a secret hole or a tunnel tucked beneath. The coyote lifted his nose to the sharp breeze one more time. The wind blew in his favor, as a creature hidden there would not smell him. He would step carefully, one paw at a time. Maybe today he would eat.

But whatever scratched or wriggled or scurried through the brush never gave away its hideout. Never poked its whiskers past the relative security of the tangled clumps of vegetation. Then silence. Hunger clawed at his insides, louder and angrier this time. A crow flapped overhead and cawed.

The coyote padded over to a rocky outcropping poking toward the blue sky. He sniffed at the cracked bark of the singleleaf pinyon jutting through the granite, twisted and bent at the knees by years of fierce winds. He lifted his head as the same wind flattened the short hairs on his back and ruffled the thicker fur around his neck. He surveyed the surrounding mountains peppered with tall pines, salted by snow. The scattered pockets of buildings closer to the valley floor, their stone chimneys piercing the roof of treetops. His gaze drifted toward the frozen lake sandwiched toward one end of the valley, its banks edged with white and silver, its once shimmering ripples encased in ice colored a steel blue, still as stone. A few stars sparkled as the day ended and the dusk deepened. Pinpricks of light twinkled across the lower sections of the valley from the buildings scattered amidst the trees.

He never strayed through the chaparral and trees carpeting the hillside to the valley floor. More people. Many more cars. He did not need to drink from the lake's deep waters. Earlier that day he had trekked to the creek that trickles from the mountain spring. He broke through a frosted plate of ice with his front paws and lapped up the icy water until he filled his belly.

Before winter, however, the lake beckoned him. He stood for brief spells, entranced, as he tuned in to the cacophony of ducks and birds that floated near the shore's edge and nested beside the water-soaked willows. But that territory belonged to another pack. He knew better than to wander away from his own. He had never tasted fresh wild duck and he never would.

A distant call made him turn his head. A human voice. Then a banging of wood against wood. He raised his muzzle and peeled his lips away from his teeth as if he could take a bite of the noise. A delicious mouse or a baby rabbit would have pleased him, but most remained burrowed in their dens to dodge the cold. No grasshoppers or crickets flitting from grass stalk to sagebrush in this blustery weather. The juniper berries either eaten or fallen to the ground and covered by dead leaves, then buried by layers of snow. He would have to hunt elsewhere for something to quiet his hunger. Toward the buildings. People often left appetizing scraps in the barrels outside of their homes, allowing a lone coyote to scrounge up a dinner out of leftovers.

Once while he and his pack cruised past the structures and hard surfaces encompassing the people, they came upon the crushed body of one of his litter mates. The pack ate what they could of her, quickly, before the lights of another car exploded, blinding them and sending them racing in all directions. Sometimes they'd corner a hissing cat. They picked off rats grown fat and lazy on scattered bird feed unless the rodent darted through a hole in a wooden shed or a stack of firewood.

And of course tantalizing aromatic bags of fruit peelings, cardboard and paper smudged with cheese and tomato sauces, half-empty containers of potato salad or chocolate pudding overflowed from the hefty bins teetering next to the streets.

He picked his way through the frozen clumps of brambles and snowdrifts toward the buildings closest to him. He peered at the collection of homes and roads he and his pack had staked as their turf. If he encountered another coyote known to him, he would warily circle it, checking if the coyote would treat him as friend or foe. Growl. Teeth bared. Hunch his shoulders and crouch ready to fight. Or maybe they would greet each other with joyful barking and yips, heralding a brief rendezvous with a like-minded being, a fellow traveler in these parts. If he came across the big one who had driven him out of the pack, the one who had torn a small but still tender gash in his leg, he'd bolt into the dark as fast as his wounded leg could carry him.

He trotted along a straightaway in the slim path, hurrying toward what he hoped would hush his hunger. As he approached the buildings, his pace slowed and he tested the breeze constantly, sniffing for threats or a possibility of food.

As he approached a wood-sided building hugging the forest, a brilliant light flicked on and he quickly withdrew back into the shadow of a massive Jeffrey pine. The scrape of wood against wood pierced the air. An explosion of human voices.

"… can't let it stink up the house, this way at least the bears won't drag my garbage bags all over the street."

"You're feeding the wildlife, bag it and store it in the freezer for trash day …"

The wood door banged shut. Then a gelatinous glob plopped onto the coyote's head. He flinched. He heard a subtle thud a few feet from his paws. Whatever hit him slid down his cheek. It smelled amazing. He licked it off, cautious at first, then with abandon. It tasted amazing. Cooked chicken fat, a tad of rubbery skin. His tongue snaked around his muzzle to capture any stray drips. He pawed his head, hoping a morsel remained somewhere on his fur. He lapped his tongue around his mouth once more and panted.

Sniffing furiously, he discovered a leg bone nearby, its rounded ends covered in gristle and cartilage. He gnawed on the bone to remove any speck of meat until he crunched it into mouthfuls he gulped down without effort. He scoured the ground for more bits of dead chicken, snuffing through dead oak leaves and brown pine needles frozen into matted clumps. His senses fired full tilt, his stomach roared. He slurped up a few dabs of fat, a hunk of roasted skin, a sliver of meat-encrusted cartilage, all devoured without chewing.

His search brought him closer to the building, into the shards of light spraying from the wall across the forest floor. He perked his ears as his nose explored, remaining cautious and listening for danger.

Pay dirt! A partial rib cage with slim strips of meat, fat and tendon rested on a large patch of snow. A hunk of skin clung to a meatier section. He snapped his jaws onto the carcass and slunk back into the darkness. He wolfed it down, chomping the bones into little chunks he swallowed with ease. He munched on a thicker section, mashing it into a pulp. A minute or so later, he licked his muzzle clean with his tongue, then sniffed at the ground for any crumbs of congealed fat dropped during his feast.

Snap. The breaking of a wooden branch in the distance snagged his attention. His muscles locked rigid. The hairs on his neck bristled upright and even the wind barely stirred them. Something was moving toward him, something in the woods lacking any fear or the need to move in stealth.

He was upwind from it, but still he arched his neck toward the sky sniffing, inhaling long and deep, to identify what plodded toward him. Slow, lumbering. A deep, low growl. The bear smelled him of course.

The coyote's senses shouted alarm and his muscles twitched into action. He sprang in the opposite direction of the growl, of the massive beast stomping over the frozen terrain toward him. Coyotes guarded against several enemies in these woods: the mountain lion, the car, sometimes other hungry coyotes. The sluggish rat stumbling blindly after ingesting a poison dispersed by humans would also sicken and oftentimes kill the coyote. Wild burros would gang up on a lone coyote and kick him to death if he got too close to their haunches, but that was rare. A young coyote, he had never seen a bear in these woods before, although he had grown familiar with their odor. As a curious youngster, he stuck his snout in their scat and caught whiffs of bear scent in a strong breeze. But he did not need any special instruction or training or advice from others in his pack. The coyote's instinct commanded him to immediately avoid any animal huge and powerful as a bear.

He sprinted haphazardly, skirting the scattered buildings before turning downward to the ravine that cut through the collection of structures. He navigated the zigzagging steep path smeared with snow and embedded with pointed rocks. His pace slowed as he crept between the crowded trees that blocked the crisp evening sky and clutched each other as if for warmth. Yesterday he had found this hollowed out mound of dead limbs and twigs entwined with tree roots that formed the faintest of shelters–a slim refuge from the harsh wind and plummeting nighttime temperatures. Snuggling himself into a ball against the farthest end, he had slept almost without fear until dawn. He would sleep there again tonight with a half-full belly. Before entering his tiny lair, he lifted his head toward the sky and released a long, mournful howl, just in case a solitary female in need of company wanted to join him.

210

THE MOUNTAINS CALLED HER NAME

Lori Brookes

She was a seer, a knower, a shaman, a medicine woman.

She was Grandmother, a member of the Serrano Tribe, Yuhaaviatam, *people of the pines*, and had lived her entire life in the Big Bear Valley, since her birth in 1890.

Her most recent grandchild was brought home from the hospital—unnamed. That was her job, to see the child, experience her, hold her up to the daylight and silhouette of the mountain, Sugarloaf, and bless her with a name.

Grandmother closed her eyes, lifted the child toward the heavens, and uttered unintelligible sounds as if communicating directly with God itself. Breaths of the child's parents were held while waiting for her mystical wisdom, the child's 'right' name. In one exhale, her heaved breath lingered—you could almost see it hang in mid-air. Lips pursed, then opened wide, like all the hearts in attendance, she proclaimed the baby girl as…

"Lilith."

Grandmother had spoken. The baby girl was ceremoniously given her name at two days young. With her eyes fixed on the child she continued, "She is a special one. Strong-willed, independent, clever, curious, and will carry forward the gifts of seeing and knowing." Lilith's proud parents had stars in their eyes at this prophetic news. Grandmother's pause was long and hard, "Her life will not be easy." She did not expand on that statement, nor explain the reason behind the name Lilith. And with that, the parents took their precious bundle home with delight and great care. She was going to need all that they could muster.

* * *

The name Lilith, from Jewish mythology, was Adam's first wife. God made them both out of the same clay and at the same time. When Adam demanded that Lilith act with subservience to him, she protested and reminded Adam that they were equals. Made from the same clay and at the same time by God. Adam did not like that and Lilith didn't care. When she left the Garden of Eden and Adam, that event sent Adam scurrying back to God to request another wife, one who would unquestioningly serve beneath him. Enter Eve. She would be made from Adam's rib, giving him some eternal leverage over her. Meanwhile, Lilith would be demonized for her bra-burning actions, leaving Eden for the mountains, and as we know Eve would also be painted in a bad light, with the whole snake and apple temptation incident. It's no wonder women are where they are today with all of the historical and fabled bad raps. And how whiny was Adam? Where's his personal responsibility in this story? No one ever talks about that. We digress.

Thankfully in later iterations of Lilith, the more modern interpretations, and through the feminist movements, she would ultimately be depicted as a strong, independent, and courageous woman warrior. Standing up for herself and fighting the good fight.

* * *

As Grandmother predicted, little Lilith was special. Quiet, shy, introspective, curious, and a precious delight to all who met her. She was observant to a fault. At a very young age, she took everything in at deep levels of feeling and knowing. She was an empath, highly tuned and sensitive… to light, sounds, smells, and touch. Not to mention the unseen interferences of voices and divine downloads of information that at times she didn't want to know.

Clairvoyance can be a dicey gift. Her visions started early, around eight years old, she would have experiences of 'nothingness', black holes, emptiness, and infinity, that would scare her too-young-to-understand self. But she did know one thing, that she couldn't ask her parents about these visions—she knew intuitively that they wouldn't have an answer for her. They were young souls and gift-less. Lilith would learn to self-resolve these experiences with the likes of Peter Pan's mantra of thinking lovely thoughts and Disney-inspired sparkles, conjuring up Cinderella and Snow White to combat her perceived darkness. Later in life, she would come to understand what she had experienced in her younger life, what she had been shown was… *where we all came from.*

* * *

The mountain environment she was born into suited her heart and soul. Lilith possessed an unmatched affinity and affection for the natural world. This is where she felt most at home. Living close to the forest's edge with the backdrop of Sugarloaf Mountain, the highest peak in the valley, this was her home, backyard playground, and where she would go to hear and feel the magic. The whispers from the forest dwellers, the tops of pine and juniper trees playing with the wind, the chatty currents of the creeks, the whooshing sounds from the winged ones, and the rustling of leaves and needles as the ground-keepers scurry from here to there. Lilith spoke that language too. She adored the scents of each season, the vanilla caramel of the Jeffrey pine bark, pine needles baked by the sun, the wet earth after a spring rain, and the clean crisp air breezed off blankets of snow. She learned to make medicine out of wild sages, junipers, and elderberries. Lilith was born to be wild, free, and in the care of the mountains.

When she wasn't out in her mountain backyard, Lilith would often be found behind the closed door to her bedroom. This is where she would read, draw, color, and write—this was also where she would escape the chaos of the household and abandon that world on the absolute other side. Lilith never understood the grievances between the parents and didn't want any part of what felt very unloving. She knew that her place in the world was much greater than what she was living. Her beloved mountain and time with the forest had taught her that.

By her early teens and much to her dismay, the parents would ultimately make a move off the mountain to the city. Devastated and not of legal age, she had no choice but to move with them. The move wasn't completely in the city, thank goodness. With a wild hair, the parents bought a California ranch, complete with barn, corrals, and a chicken coop. They tried to appease her mountain melancholy with a horse. Her name was Honey. She was a rather large quarter horse, standing 18 hands high, that's how you measure a horse—but whose hands? She was so tall and broad that Lilith never used a saddle on her, just a bareback pad. A gentle giant she came to love, who would take her up and over the hills across the dirt road, far away from the continued and strengthened madness, the tumultuous relationship between her parents.

Some sense of sanity came in as Lilith carved out an independent life during her high school years. She was a straight-A student, well-liked by her teachers, she enjoyed her loving friends and social life, and she also had a penchant for connecting with the downtrodden. The kids in her school that the others shunned, bullied, or worse. As her independence and world grew so did the element of *wrong people, and wrong actions.* She mourned her experiences of robbed innocence in silence and craved the return to her place in the mountains evermore.

At long last, legal adulthood arrived, and just as soon as the candles were blown out and smoldering on her 18th birthday cake, Lilith returned to her former life in the mountains of Big Bear.

Serendipitously, Grandmother had not only passed her ethereal gifts to Lilith, but in her life passing, she had bequeathed her mountain cabin on the eastern edge of the valley known as Erwin Lake to Lilith.

In her first year of return as a *people of the pines*, and Grandmother's prodigy, Lilith sifted through all of the left-behinds from the wise woman. She felt a strangeness about the sense of familiarity and connection with Grandmother's belongings. Belongings... a belonging. Yes, that was it! Lilith knew she belonged in this valley and larger still was the strong tie to her Grandmother and Grandmother's gifts from, through, and with the world of spirit.

The cabin was small in footprint, built with a simplicity that spoke to Lilith's soul, an almost off-the-grid situation. This gave her an even greater sense of connectedness to the forest and mountains. She would not change a thing. A chosen lifestyle of 'chop wood—carry water,' a lesson she had learned through self-seeking studies of Eastern Philosophy while living down the mountain that fell in alignment with her people. She was home.

Lilith lived a revered life solo in the mountains. She was known as the go-to expert for all things forest, the truth-teller of sordid history bits from the Big Bear Valley, the flora and fauna, and all of the precious wildlife within. The latter were her true friends.

From her humble abode on the East side, the people of Big Bear would seek her out, just like Grandmother for all things healing. The gift that was passed down, skipped her mother and grew stronger in Lilith as each year passed in reverence and through the flowing elegance of each of the four seasons. Her wisdom and clairvoyance grew as the veil thinned.

Different from her Grandmother, Lilith also worked with all sentient beings, for the most part, that meant the domesticated beings. Not that she didn't have an occasional encounter with the beings in the wild. You've no doubt heard of *the whisperers,* the highly sensitive people who connect with and understand animals without the use of the spoken word… Lilith was one of them.

Once a sweet pit bull who lived across the street with a bad human, who was often visited by the local Sheriffs, with their megaphones blaring and guns drawn, would often escape and run over to her cabin.

She knew he did not want to go back home, but all she could do was listen and soothe his fears. "You can always come over here, buddy."

His name was Chunk, all white except for the splat of black fur on top of his broadly shaped head. His 'owner' named him Chunk because of that prominent marking. One day as Lilith was driving home, Chunk came running out of the forest and straight for her car, as if he'd been waiting for that divine timing. She opened the door and saw that Chunk was without his spiked collar and in an extremely stressed state. He had escaped. Chunk, through his overheated panting and tongue dragging, had told her that he had escaped and did not want to go back to that man. And if she didn't do something about it, he would run right back into the forest and take his chances in the wild. In that fine-line moment, Lilith gave him the get-in signal and Chunk, without hesitation, hopped into her car. When she saw that his 'owner' was not home, she drove him to the shelter, explained his situation to her friend who ran the place, and the shelter took over from there.

It turned out his keeper was not the legal owner, gratefully he was chipped which revealed that and more information about his sordid life with humans. The owners of record gave up their rights to him and the shelter renamed him Chuck, hid his presence at the shelter from the man who unrightfully claimed him, and ultimately found Chuck a new and loving life. Lilith had wanted to adopt Chunk/Chuck, but proximity made that impossible. This would be one of many experiences of profound connection that Lilith would have with the animal world. They loved her and she loved them all right back.

Her life on the mountain was truly divine. Filled with connections to all good people, a sustainable livelihood that was of high value, all surrounded by an abundance of beauty and ease. Life was always good. That is how she chose to see and live. She came from the *people of the pines*, lived closely to their ways, with paralleled Buddhist precepts, and lived out Zen proverbs such as; before enlightenment, chop wood—carry water; after enlightenment, chop wood—carry water. Lilith strived to live with the absence of ego and a richness in simplicity and living-loving kindness.

* * *

She was a seer, a knower, a shaman, a medicine woman.

Silver-haired and with a beautiful face creased in deep lines from both the frailty and fullness of life, Lilith felt complete with her earthly destiny, and rather than being relegated to one of those life-diminishing old folks' homes, she set out on a solo walkabout into the wild, the place she was so completely connected and felt enormously loved and held.

Lilith chuckled to herself as she recalled the time she told a close friend her plan, her plan for when the end was near, and how she would climb the mountain with no return ticket. It would be a peacefully perfect exit, a true final communion with Mother Nature and the ancestors. She never feared the wild, and she looked forward to this hike.

Her friend had listened without judgment or scrunched-up facial expressions, but what he heard, as told back by him a few years later, which she had to immediately correct, "No! I never said we'd hike up the mountain together and then you'd push me off!!! No, no, no!"

To say the least, he was relieved. What a horrible friend she would have been to make that kind of request! This would be of her own accord, place, and select time.

That day had come, all felt right and completed with her life, and Lilith stood at the base of the highest peak in the valley, Sugarloaf. The wind blew her long gray strands clear from her face, her eyes closed in mindful meditation as she faced the sun, waited, and listened with a wide smile of surrender until she heard the mountains call her name.

POWER OUTAGE

Christie Walker Bos

It was indeed a dark and stormy night with a howling wind pushing the clouds up the canyon, over the dam, and into Big Bear Valley. For over an hour, the snow fell, but not the gentle soft powder that covered the landscape with a soft blanket of white … this snow had teeth with crystalline shards of ice tapping on the windows like Morse code.

Rebecca placed another strip of limp pasta on the lasagna, before sprinkling the completed casserole with a final layer of cheese. Dinner in the oven, timer set for an hour, Rebecca poured herself a glass of red wine, leaned back against the kitchen counter, and surveyed the mess she'd created.

Maybe I'll ask the kids to clean this up before dinner, she thought, then chuckled at the absurdity of the thought. The complaints she'd have to endure would negate any reprieve from avoiding the task.

She texted her two teenagers, Sean and Aubry, who were upstairs engrossed in whatever it was teenagers did. Her message of "Dinner in an hour" was answered with emojis … a thumbs up, a red heart, and a casserole pan from Sean; a thumbs up, a pink smiley face, and two hearts from Aubry.

Whatever happened to using words, Rebecca thought before the phone rang. Were the kids actually calling her? Caller ID showed, "Husband." A quick check of the time made her realize that Jack should have been home hours ago. She'd been so caught up making dinner that she hadn't noticed the time.

She answered the phone with, "Are you okay?"

"I'm fine," came her husband's voice, although the crackling of interference made it difficult to catch all his words. "The 330 is closed. Rockslides along the Arctic Circle. I started up the 38 and made it all the way to Onyx Summit, only to find traffic has been stopped for over an hour. Some idiot tried coming up without chains, slid into another idiot without chains, and then a semi-truck plowed into them both. No one was hurt but the semi is sideways on the road. Highway Patrol is turning everyone around."

"What about the desert side?"

"I heard it's a mess, too. I'll get a hotel for the night. Try again in the morning."

"Okay. Love you," she was able to say before they lost the connection.

Back in the kitchen, she took a healthy sip of wine before turning on the hot water. Then, as if someone had flipped a switch, the power went out and the house descended into darkness. Like fire sprinklers popping on at the first sign of smoke, her kids came stomping down the stairs, using the flashlights on their phones to light the way.

"The power's out," they shouted in tandem as if she hadn't noticed.

Rebecca had to bite her lip to stop herself from saying, "Really?"

"How long will it be out?" asked fourteen-year-old Aubry as if her mom could predict the future.

Power outages during snowstorms were as common as tourists getting stuck in the snow. It wasn't a matter of "if" there would be an outage, but "how long" would it last.

"Is it just our house or the whole neighborhood," sixteen-year-old Sean wanted to know.

"That's a good question. Why don't you go outside and check? See if the neighbors' lights are on. Aubry and I will light some candles."

Once the first six candles were lit, Aubry switched off her flashlight and plopped on the couch as her mother moved around the room lighting the rest. The golden glow of a dozen candles imbued the room with a visual warmth if not a physical one.

"It looks beautiful."

Aubry looked up from her phone for a hot second, and said a single word, "Yeah," before returning to flipping through posts on Instagram.

"You know, you might want to turn that off. I don't know how long the power will be out and then we'll have no way to charge our phones."

That got her attention. Aubry peered at the battery icon on her phone. Twenty percent. "What are you going to do? I need my phone."

The urgency in Aubry's voice made Rebecca sigh. "You don't *need* your phone. What we do need is a fire because it's going to get cold in here without the heater."

Aubry looked at her mother like she was speaking a foreign language. Rebecca shook her head. How could her daughter be so clueless? This wasn't the first time the power had gone out.

"Everything in this house runs on electricity. No

electricity, no heat. Now turn off your phone and help me bring firewood in from the garage."

Now it was Aubry's turn to sigh.

The front door flew open along with Sean and a blast of cold air and snow that dusted the hardwood floor of the entryway like powdered sugar sprinkled on a golden waffle.

"Close the door," Aubry shouted. "We have no heat."

Sean ignored his sister. "The lights are out everywhere. It's like totally dark out there. I mean really dark."

"Okay, then. Everyone is in the same boat, so we need to get ready for a long cold night. Come on. Let's bring in firewood from the garage. Hopefully, there will be enough, and we won't have to hike out to the woodshed."

For the next fifteen minutes, Rebecca and the kids shuttled armful after armful of firewood into the house. Kneeling on a cushion in front of the fireplace,

Rebecca crumpled newspaper and then created an interlocking log cabin-like structure over the paper.

"Your dad usually does this. He says that based on the history of hundreds of cabins burning to the ground in Big Bear, he's concluded that the log cabin wood stack is the most reliable way to start a fire."

When no one acknowledged her comment, Rebecca looked over her shoulder to find both kids on the couch, the light of their cell phones illuminating their faces. "You should turn off your phones. We don't have a way to charge them. We might need them later for an emergency."

"This *is* an emergency. Everyone is texting about the blackout. Marcie's parents have a generator so she can charge her phone. Why don't *we* have a generator?" Aubry asked, with a whine.

Good question, Rebecca thought, but decided to let it go, turning back to the task at hand. With the miniature log cabin three rows high, she lit a match and touched it to the newspaper. It didn't take long for the entire structure to start smoking and then as if by magic, burst into flames.

Rebecca let out a little, "Woop! Did you see that?" She turned to the kids. "The log cabin method works."

"Great," said Sean, although she could tell that he could care less.

Maybe he'll care more when the temperature drops and they need the fire to keep warm, Rebecca thought as she pushed herself up to a stand.

"I'm hungry," Aubry announced without looking up from her phone.

"Me too," agreed Sean. "I'm guessing we aren't having lasagna. What are we going to eat?"

Were her kids really this helpless? How had she not noticed before? Rebecca looked at the cell phones in their hands and imagined their brains being sucked out of their heads and into their phones like a scene from a sci-fi movie. She'd had enough.

"If you want to eat, you'll need to turn off your phones and join me in the kitchen. We have food in this house that doesn't need to be cooked. Let's figure it out together." Rebecca grabbed two candles and headed for the kitchen.

It took—what seemed like an eternity—for the kids to comprehend and act. First Sean, then reluctantly, Aubry, shut their phones off, and join her in the kitchen.

"You guys go through the pantry and pull out anything we can eat that doesn't have to be cooked. Spread it out on the island so we can see our options. I'll see what we have in the fridge."

Moments later, they stood around the island in the glow of the candles surveying their collection … peanut butter, jelly, cheese, three types of crackers, almonds and sunflower seeds, celery, cream cheese, a package of turkey lunch meat, mini oranges, grapes, one banana, a loaf of sourdough bread, and a bag of dark chocolate squares.

Rebecca nodded with satisfaction. They certainly were not going to starve. "What we have here will make an excellent charcuterie."

"A what?" the kids asked in unison.

"Charcuterie. Adults put them together for parties. It's basically a fancy snack tray," Rebecca explained. "I'll take care of the food. Why don't you clear a space in front of the fireplace where we can eat."

To Rebecca's surprise, the kids didn't argue and headed back into the living room. While she assembled and cut PB&J sandwiches into elegant triangles, peeled and separated the oranges into sections, cut the banana into thin slices, then drizzled them with Hershey's chocolate, rolled the lunch meat around sticks of cheese, spread cream cheese on pieces of celery, and arranged it artfully on a large cutting board, Rebecca could hear the sound of furniture being dragged across the floor and some good-natured arguing over/about how close they wanted to be to the fireplace.

When she walked into the living room, the tray of food held in her hands, she smiled at the sight of what the kids had created. The couch and coffee table were now positioned directly in front of the fireplace instead of in front of the TV, with the coffee table cleared of its customary collection of magazines and electronics. Six candles of varying heights gathered together like a little family providing enough light to see what they were about to eat.

"Good job. This looks perfect," Rebecca said, setting the large cutting board in the center of the table.

Sean came closer to examine his dining options, "You made all of this from the stuff we found?" he asked, picking up one of the chocolate-drizzled banana slices.

Rebecca shrugged. The book club wouldn't have been impressed but as long as her kids were happy, that was all that mattered.

"Looks good," Aubry conceded, grabbing a celery stick with cream cheese.

"Sean. Can you help me with plates and napkins?"

Sean followed his mom into the kitchen and returned moments later with three plates and a stack of napkins. The sound of a cork popping had both kids turning around. Rebecca reentered the room with three crystal champagne flutes and a bottle of bubbly.

"You're letting us drink champagne," Aubry asked, her eyes big with astonishment.

"Sparkling cider. Non-alcoholic," Rebecca said, setting a flute in front of each plate.

"Figures. I knew you weren't *that* cool," Aubry mumbled under her breath.

Rebecca heard and ignored the comment, pouring the amber liquid into each glass. "Who's sitting where?"

"Sit in the middle, Mom. That way I don't have to sit next to the grouch," Sean said, making a face at his sister.

"You're the one who said the shacutteray-thing was going to be lame."

Doing her best to ignore their bickering, Rebecca took her place on the middle cushion of the three-cushion couch and waited for the kids to sit down next to her. She would have loved to have poured herself another glass of wine, curl up next to the fire, and read her book by firelight, but instead, she was the wall that kept her kids from harassing each other.

The food disappeared faster than the fire, to which Rebecca added two more logs. Aubry waited a full minute before asking with boredom dripping off every word, "What are we going to do now?"

"We could read," Rebecca suggested, knowing the idea would never fly.

"Boring," they both said together.

"How about a game?"

"What game? All of our games are on our phones," Aubry said with a defeated sigh.

Rebecca stood and walked over to the coat closet. Standing on tiptoes, she pulled down a box. The dust from the top of the box made her sneeze. She placed the game on the coffee table before bringing over a dining room chair so she could sit across from the kids.

"Monopoly? I remember this game," Sean said as he lifted the lid, revealing the game board and a stack of colorful money.

"Never heard of it," Aubry proclaimed, arms crossed over her chest, determined not to have any fun.

Rebecca added another log to the fire and then took a seat. "By the time you were old enough to play, you guys weren't interested in board games anymore."

Rebecca pulled a baggie of little metal game pieces out from under the wad of money and dumped them in her hand. "Pick."

Aubry snatched the Scottie dog and Sean took the car.

"Your Dad was always the car," Rebecca said, as she took the hat, before dropping the remaining pieces in the box. "I'll be the bank. We each start with $1500."

Over the next two hours, the hat, the car, and the Scottie dog traveled around the board, collecting $200, occasionally landing in jail, buying property, and paying taxes. Good-natured ribbing over money due when someone landed on a property with a hotel, had pasted a smile on Rebecca's face that hadn't been there in who knows how long. Sean, the land baron, as they started calling him, kept landing on all the high-end rents. He owned everything from Pacific Avenue to Boardwalk and all the properties in between. You couldn't make it down that side of the board without paying Sean something, which infuriated Aubry. When Aubry got down to her last $100, Rebecca sent Sean to the kitchen for drinks, slipping Aubry a wad of cash before Sean returned.

"Thanks, Mom. I wish this wasn't fake money," she said with a gleam in her eye, hiding the new bills under her beige one-hundred-dollar bill.

Sean had just landed on the Go to Jail corner, causing Aubry to shout with joy, when the lights blinked on, and the heater whooshed to life. Both kids cheered, popped up, grabbed their phones, and rushed to the stairs, disappearing in a matter of seconds.

Rebecca sighed. Three hours electronics-free. No emails, text messages, or looking at social media until your eyes burn. It had been wonderful and now it was over, like flipping a switch. Rising, she walked around the living room blowing out the candles. Even though the fire still blazed, the room had lost its magic.

Returning to the board game, Rebecca began dividing her money by color. As she picked up Sean's stack of bills, she heard, "Hey, that's mine."

Rebecca looked up in time to see Sean jump off the last stair, Aubry on his heels. "Are we still playing?"

Sean plopped on the couch, taking the money from Rebecca's hand. "Yeah. I'm winning."

"Not for long." Aubry took her place on the opposite side of the couch.

"You left, so I thought …"

"We went to plug our phones in," said Sean.

"So we'd have full power, in case of an emergency. You should probably plug in your phone, too," Aubry suggested, sounding very grown up.

Still in shock, Rebecca made her way to the kitchen. She plugged in her phone, checked to see if there was a message from Jack, and then decided to make hot chocolate. When she returned, Sean and Aubry were acting oddly. Then she noticed that their stacks of money were a bit thicker, and the bank stacks were a bit thinner.

She decided to let them get away with their thievery, setting a cup of cocoa in front of each of them, and asking, "Okay. Whose turn was it?"

But before Rebecca could sit down, Aubry asked, "Can we light the candles again? It's so bright with all the lights on."

"And more wood in the fire," Sean added. "The heater is too loud."

Rebecca's mouth dropped open. Who were these strange children? No cell phones. No lights. No heater.

"Thank you, power outage," Rebecca whispered under her breath as she walked around the room lighting the candles. The kitchen light flickered, which Rebecca interpreted as, "Anytime."

A CLICK AWAY

Yvonne Phillips

Making a wine cellar in the boulders that
surround my home was a long process. Finally
finished, I needed to share my success with someone,
and turning to the internet fed my ego.

I like women. I especially like women on the Internet.
They seem to lose their inhibitions when there, like
they're on vacation. They'll tell you anything when
you chat them up for a while and ask the right
questions.

"Writer desperately needs a critique partner. You show me yours and I'll show you mine." Is a line I use quite often. It usually results in a ha-ha from women who are only cruising the Internet. But always receives a notable response from other writers, men included. Everyone wants their work critiqued.

Of course, only the women interest me, but I scan the men's writing and generate polite noncommittal replies. Only a few press further.

Most women take the time to help me, always a good sign. They patiently explain there are websites for beginning authors, and that's where I ought to look. The conversations usually go something like this.

"Timmy, there are websites for folks like you. I'm sure you can find help there."

"Oh, I didn't realize. Thanks for the tip. Are you a writer?"

"Well, I dabble a bit, but I have published nothing yet."

"What do you write?"

"Romance, mostly. A little poetry sometimes."

"Romance, that's interesting. We're two birds of a feather; we ought to stick together." I chuckled and wiped my sweating palms on my pants. "Do you write Hallmark-style romances? You know, a kiss goodnight at the front door?"

Almost all admit to wanting and writing a little more, some a lot more, than only a kiss at the door. I can usually start the culling process from their answers to my simple question. And that's when my fun begins.

Usually, my process nets three or four serious respondents. I send them a simple sample of a few pages that have obvious errors. Passive voice, head hopping, change of point of view mid-paragraph, and sit back and wait. Of course, all of this is prefaced with a meek woe is me. "I know this isn't very good," type of confession from me.

For this process, Private Messenger is best. These women must never know about each other. If I don't choose them this time, maybe they'll make the cut next time. Who knows?

These few women seldom disappoint. They'll point out my errors with articles on how to improve. This can lead to long online discussions. These are the most beneficial. They don't feel threatened, only helpful. They see me as a "student," they can help. Works every time.

Next comes the time for them to share their writing with me. Some are quite good, a few not so much. I start with the ones that flounder, pointing them to free workshops and online lessons. Gently correcting their work and suggesting a better way to say something. To a one they are grateful. And I count on that.

I enjoy the interaction with the better writers. They're more confident and resist some things I suggest. Resistance is good. I like a woman with spirit, just not too much spirit.

My better writings get sent their way and they usually have interesting comments and edits. Some are accepted and others get rejected. These are not the women I want in my inner circle, but I want to keep them in my stable of writer friends to call on if need be.

It's a long process, but worth it in the end. I shall call the lessor writers newbies and give them each a name.

Stella is a divorced mother of two college-aged kids and has a nothing-to-speak-of job to help pay the bills. Same ole story. Her husband left her for a younger woman. Stella got the house and all the expenses that go with it. She wants to keep it because it's the "family" home and if her kids ever come home on school break, they'll feel 'at home.' However, they never visit.

My second newbie is Nancy. A name right out of the forties. I looked it up. Once it was in the ten most popular girls' names from the 1930s to 1955. And Nancy is just as old-fashioned as her name. She's a bookkeeper for several smaller businesses and works from home. No boyfriend, no family, and with grocery delivery, she seldom leaves the house. So far, she's the leading candidate.

Lastly, there's Teri. Much more modern than the other two. Writes contemporary romance. Is wise to the ways of the world. She's hungry for romance and not afraid to put it out there. We exchanged numbers, and I called her.

"So, tell me, Timmy, are you married?" Her voice was low and throaty, sounding movie sexy.

I lied and told her I was, and that I wasn't here for a romantic fling, online or otherwise. She sent me some of her writings, they bordered on Erotica. Then she sent me a picture. One of those 'instant glamor photos' that make even the plainest Jane look enticing. She was definitely a keeper. I saved her picture and writing in the HOT file. It had dwindled in size over the past year or so.

It didn't take long to decide. For my purposes, I chose Nancy. No family, no friends to dissuade her from meeting someone she'd only met online, even if just for coffee or tea.

Lucky for me, we didn't live too great a distance from each other. I lived in a rustic mountain cabin in Big Bear. She lived in a small apartment in Pasadena. I bragged about my wine cellar made into the mountainside guarded by giant boulders; she was impressed. She bragged about her computing skills. The two-hour commute was doable, for a once a once-a-week or an every-two-week dating schedule.

After chatting online for several weeks, I suggested a phone call. We traded numbers, and I called her.

"Hello."

Her voice matched the mental image I'd conjured up.

"Nancy? This is Tim. How are you today? How's the story coming along?"

"I'm good, thanks. You called at just the right time. I need your advice about how to phrase something. You must have a sixth sense."

"I'll be glad to help you with whatever you need. You know I'm always just a click away. Say, I have to be down your way next week and was wondering if you'd like to meet up for a cup of tea. I know a great little place on Green Street. You can bring your computer and we can go over your manuscript. I sure hope you say yes. I'd love to meet you."

Silence and shuffling of papers. "Nancy, are you still there?"

"Yes, I'm here. What day and time do you want to meet I need to check my calendar?"

"Tuesday, my doctor's appointment is Tuesday morning at ten."

"Are you sick? Did you take a Covid test? I don't want to catch anything. That's part of the reason I don't go out much."

"No, no. It's nothing like that. It's an old war injury. The docs need to check it every so often. Just a routine check-up, that's all. I'll text you the address of the tea shop. Do you know where Green Street is?"

"Yes, Tim, I know where it is. I can be there by eleven. Is that good for you?"

"It sure is. I can't wait to meet you. See you Tuesday."

* * *

Carolyn Duffy, Homicide Detective, hung up the phone and looked at her partner, Detective Andy Thomas, and smiled. "He bit. He wants to meet 'Nancy' next week at the tea shop on Green."

Andy nodded. "I knew you could pull this off." Tim, real name Jordan Stevens, had fallen easily into their trap. "I thought for sure he'd fall for Teri, the sex goddess. But you were right; he wanted someone meek and unsure of herself. It's about time. We've been working on this Computer Casanova case for months."

"The sheriffs in Big Bear have eyes on him. They'll let us know when he crosses the dam. We'll have two hours to get everyone in place. This arrest is going down with no hitches. He's already killed four women, and he's not adding Nancy to his total. I wouldn't be surprised if they find bodies in that mountain wine cellar of his."

252

Lori Brookes

An accomplished writer, published author, and award-winning photographer, Lori published her first slice-in-time memoir in 2020, *The Unintended Positive Consequences of Hiking.* Her memoir chronicles her journey as a newbie hiker which she called The Sixty60 Journey. Sixty hikes to 60 years: a year-long endeavor that spanned the time between her 59th and 60th birthdays. Lori's prior career in marketing as a Creative Director allowed her to use her skills as writer, photographer, and designer in creating this book.

Her previous published works are a series of coffee-table style books, *Shadows & Reflections* and *In Living Contrast*, in which she blends her passion for photography and writing, with philosophical musings that accompany each of her images. The anthology, *Big Bear Tales*, is Lori's first dive into writing fictionalized short stories or what she calls "altered truths." Originally from San Diego, she now lives in Big Bear. The mountains called and she went.

Lori's memoir is available on Amazon and her photo essay books can be purchased at Blurb.com. You can follow her on Facebook at LoriBrookesAuthor.

Christie Walker Bos

"A writer is who I am."
Writer, photographer, and editor, Christie Walker Bos has worn many hats in her 40-plus-year writing career. A published author in both fiction and non-fiction, Christie has lived in Big Bear since 2001, working from home in Baldwin Lake, which keeps her inspired and creative. Her published novels include three romantic comedies available as e-books: *Magical Man List, The Write Man for Her,* and *Getting Back to Delaney;* a contemporary women's fiction, *Fearless,* and two stories inspired by Big Bear ... a murder mystery, *The Community Garden ... more than the tomatoes are dying,* and the follow-up novel, *No Words Between Us.* Christie's next novel is based on a road trip she took with her best friend and explores the grieving process and how grief, like a road trip, is full of ups and downs, discoveries, and surprises.

Check out her novels and sign up for her newsletter at ChristieWalkerBos.com. Contact her at christiewalkerbos@gmail.com. Her novels are for sale on Amazon, and also on Audible.

Yvonne Phillips

 Yvonne Phillips is the published author of nine novels. Her stories cross genres from Contemporary Romance to Mystery/Thrillers. She began her writing career at age seventy and hasn't looked back. Yvonne and her husband Don married young, very young, dropping out of high school after tenth grade. She graduated college when her children were teenagers, worked for twenty-five years at the telephone company, retired, and then had an antique business for fifteen years.

A voracious reader as a child, her love of reading continued into adulthood. One day, after reading an unsatisfying book, she said aloud, "I can write a book better than this," and so she did, nine of them. Four of her novels take place in and around Paso Robles wine country, three in Big Bear, one in both Paso Robles and Big Bear, and the latest in Colorado. Yvonne and Don moved to Big Bear from their San Fernando Valley home twenty-five years ago. They are active in community affairs, and two of their four adult grandchildren also live in Big Bear.

Her books are on Amazon, and several times a year, she does book signings in Big Bear and Paso Robles.

Karene Horst

As a fourth grader, Karene Horst decided she wanted to be a writer when she grew up, and it's been downhill ever since.

Karene is a contributing editor for GonzoToday.com, an online magazine on culture, politics, and music. Her first novel, **Moving Men,** is a psychological thriller set in the Ozarks. **Moving Men** has won a Wishing Shelf Book Award and an Honorable Mention from Royal Dragonfly Book Awards.

To mix fact with fiction for her Big Bear Tales, Karene relied on: Ryan Orr, Director of Marketing & Business Development, and Laura Gehr MSN, RN Clinical Data Analyst, at Bear Valley Community Healthcare District; Brian Parham, Battalion Chief and EMS Coordinator for Big Bear Fire Department; Connor Renard, Natural Resource Specialist for the San Bernardino National Forest Service; locals Herb Potter for sharing armfuls of books and Cheryle Potter for her editing expertise; and the writer's group with the Big Bear Chapter of the American Association of University Women, which inspired the first few paragraphs of "Coyote Day."

A Californian by birth and by choice, Karene spent her childhood in Santa Monica. She moved to the Midwest to finish college and wound up in the Ozarks for three decades. When not traveling in her van to the beach and around North America or wandering out of the country, Karene now lives and plays in the mountains of Southern California snowboarding, skiing, hiking, kayaking, and mountain biking while dodging rattlesnakes and wildfires.

Read more from Karene or contact her via:
flyingtreespublishing.com/karene-horst
flyingtreespublishing@gmail.com
Facebook @authorkarenehorst

Thanks for Reading!